The Life in Death

The Life in Death

Ann & Michele Modtland

Desert Palm Press

The Life in Death
By Ann & Michele Modtland

©2019 Ann & Michele Modtland

ISBN (trade) 9781948327534
ISBN (epub) 9781948327541
SBN (pdf) 9781948327558

Desert Palm Press
1961 Main Street, Suite 220
Watsonville, California 95076
www.desertpalmpress.com

Editor: Nat Burns
Cover Design: Ann McMan, TreeHouse Studio

Printed in the United States of America
First Edition December 2019

Dedication

To our beautiful Daughter
and
to our loved ones, seen and unseen.

.

PROLOGUE

My Last Breath

LOOKING DOWN AT YOUR dying body is indescribable, yet terrifying and unnatural. I saw my body shaking as my brain delivered its final electrical impulses, my back arching as it desperately sought life-giving air. As I reached down in a frantic attempt to put myself back together, the seizure suddenly stopped. Blood pooled from the hole in my head— a much larger amount than I had expected. Anxious to save myself, I instinctively tried to push the blood back through the hole, but I couldn't grasp anything. I was intangible. There was a gurgling, moaning sound as my breath left my body. Then everything went still. I panicked and repeatedly tried to get back into my body, but it was useless. My life was finished and my soul—me—had been freed from the confines of the physical world. It was done. There was no going back. I was dead.

My death should not have been a surprise, at least not to me. For weeks, I had researched the connections between the physical and spiritual worlds. I understood the importance of symbolism, dates, times, energy, and our thoughts before death. I had prepared for everything. I made sure my finances and legal documents were in proper order for my parents to care for my beloved dog, Chewy. I packed up the house to alleviate any stress my family might have when going through my things. I gave the baby's furniture to my cousin who was seven months pregnant. I made sure my relationships were all in good standing. I even washed my car. I wanted to leave no loose ends.

But, despite all that groundwork, the horror of seeing my body fighting for life was a shock. I had never considered the power of one's strong will to live, nor had I anticipated how frightening it would be when witnessing the last signs of life leaving my body. Now that body was lying, limp and lifeless in the snow, appearing almost as if it were a stranger, some other woman's body. I tried to comprehend how my soulless body could look so different from how I had appeared in life. My shoulder-length brown hair was now saturated in blood. My eyes, eyes through which I had viewed the world around me every day, stared emptily, blankly. The body that had sheltered my soul for the past thirty-three years was now just a shell. It wasn't me anymore.

Nonetheless, I felt a tremendous feeling of responsibility, of love and devotion toward that body. It had served my spirit well and supported me during a mostly wonderful life in the physical world. I needed to make sure it was attended to. I knew it deserved at least that much respect. I felt compelled to stay with it until it had been properly cared for. And a part of me also acknowledged shame for what I had done. I prayed my body, my family, my friends would forgive me.

CHAPTER ONE

January Third

IT WAS PRECISELY NINE thirteen on the evening of the third day in January when I pulled the trigger—at the same place and time Bryndle's body had been discovered just three years before. It was freezing cold. I had only been in the woods a few moments before my fingers and toes turned numb. Although it was snowing heavily, the dense forest gave me some refuge. And though there was no escape from the cold, I trembled mostly from fear as I prepared to take that final, irreversible step.

It had only been a few weeks since I had learned the unimaginable and questioned everything I once believed. That knowledge forced me into a decision no one should face, much less contemplate. Taking your life goes against your very nature, no matter the reasons you use to convince yourself of the validity, the morality, the necessity of that act. No amount of planning can change that. As the critical time approached, I wasn't sure I possessed the courage to pull the trigger. But I did.

I had spent weeks, days, hours considering other ways to cross over, ways to ensure a death that wouldn't be so hard on my body. However, with a gun—once I overcame the fear of pulling the trigger— my death would be assured. And when it came down to that final moment, I was petrified. As I held the gun in my mouth, it shook against my teeth. A million reasons why I shouldn't do it flooded my mind. I told myself that no matter what fears I had; they were nothing compared to hers. Thoughts of Bryndle gave me the courage to overcome those fears and to pull the trigger.

I thought that act would be the most difficult part, but it wasn't. After my death, I was beset with a complex series of emotions. I had to find Bryndle, but I was reluctant to leave my body alone in the night. It looked so helpless, so betrayed. I wasn't sure what to do next. I called out for guidance, but there was no response. I was alone in the dark forest with my body.

Ann and Michele Modtland

CHAPTER TWO

The Reunion

FEELINGS OF DREAD FILLED the quiet of the night and I wondered, had I done all of this for nothing? Had I come to the wrong conclusion? Would I be able to help Bryndle? Hopelessness, unlike anything I had experienced before, surrounded me in a thick heavy darkness.

What have I done? I dropped to my knees in despair. Then, a tremendous light surrounded me. It was a brilliant white, simultaneously filled with life, energy, and emotion. With it came an overwhelming feeling of love, acceptance, warmth, and safety. Every particle of that light was love.

The light filled me with strength, and I rose from my knees. I saw several people approaching. Somehow, they glowed, shining even brighter than the surrounding light itself. As my eyes focused on the figures, I recognized my grandma. Yet she was so young and beautiful, her dark curly hair and brown eyes surprisingly youthful. I had never seen my grandma this way, and I hadn't realized how much I resembled her. Years of battling cancer had left her tired and frail toward the end of her life. My last memories of her were after chemotherapy had weakened her. Her eyes had become sunken and her skin a pasty gray. Now, remarkably, she stood before me healthy, vibrant, and strong. Snuggled in her arms was a beautiful baby I was instantly drawn to.

I suddenly recognized this little spirit as my beloved Oryan. I had felt her spirit fill our home when Bryndle was pregnant with her. After their deaths I could feel Oryan's spirit comfort me from time to time. Smiling, my grandma lovingly handed me my baby girl. I couldn't believe it, here she was lying safely in my arms, just as I had envisioned she would, once born.

"Oh, my gosh, my baby girl. Oryan, you're so beautiful," I whispered.

She was so precious and tiny, with soft curly hair and big blue eyes that were just like my beautiful Bryndle's. I cried tears of absolute joy. I was holding my precious baby, my unborn child, the precious soul I feared I would never meet—all because she was taken away from me before she was born. I had never believed I would have the opportunity to see her, let alone hold her. Holding her changed me instantly—a broken part of me healed from my expanding feelings of love.

Thad and Louise, Bryndle's parents, were there, too, and smiled lovingly at me as they watched me hold their granddaughter. They had passed in a car accident when Bryndle was a teenager, but I would have recognized them anywhere from all the pictures Bryndle had placed throughout our house. She had adored her parents. Her appearance was a mix of them both. She had blond hair and large blue eyes just like her mom and was slender with a flawless smile like her dad. It was an honor to meet them for the first time. They embraced me as I held baby Oryan. No one said anything. There was no need.

CHAPTER THREE

Choices

ANOTHER FIGURE APPEARED ALONGSIDE Bryndle's parents—a man I didn't recognize, although he felt familiar somehow. He had dark, perfect skin, and the kindest eyes I had ever seen. He watched me intently and, as he stepped forward, everyone else respectfully stepped back. I looked away as I cradled Oryan in my arms, gently rocking her back and forth. I was mesmerized by every inch of her. Her little nose and chubby cheeks, the way she moved her mouth—she was perfect, and I couldn't take my eyes off her. It was difficult to acknowledge anyone else. I was lost in Oryan, examining her delicate fingers and toes. I loved the way she smelled and the softness of her skin.

My name is Michael. The man spoke in a powerful voice that demanded my immediate attention. *You have taken a drastic step choosing to advance the time of your soul's passage. Another choice lies before you, Tallon. It is yours alone to make. We have come to invite you to the light. However, knowing you as I do, I don't believe that is your plan. If you decide to continue the journey you have chosen, you will have to complete it alone. If you do, know that the universe is full of energy—the highest being pure love, which is our goal to obtain, and the lowest is the absence of love. There are also many variations and vibrations in between. Light and dark are both powerful.*

Let me give you a piece of advice, Tallon. Be careful choosing which energy source you use on your journey, for it will become part of your being and thus impact your eternal life. You carry a power you do not yet understand. Please remember to look within before you embark. The decision is yours and you need to choose wisely—and remember, as with all choices, there is something to lose and something to gain.

My mind raced. How could this stranger know me? And what energy was he talking about? I was confused, longing to stay with my family. Even so, I knew my family was incomplete. Bryndle, my love, was not there.

Can I take her with me? I asked, holding Oryan tighter. Now that I had found her, how could I let her go? How could I leave her? Oryan was finally in my arms and now I was being forced to make another impossible choice. I just wanted to take her and run, but I knew I couldn't. I looked pleadingly into Michael's eyes.

No, he answered.

I hesitated, torn between being with my baby and keeping the promise to save my wife from an eternal hell. I looked back at my body, my dead hand still clenching the photo of Bryndle and me. We had looked so happy then.

My decision was made. Leaving Bryndle behind wasn't an option. This was my last chance to make things right. I handed my beloved baby girl back to my grandma, tears streaming down my face.

I have to go help mommy, and we will all be together soon, I lovingly explained to Oryan, as I stroked her cheek and kissed her tiny forehead.

In truth, I didn't know if I would ever see Oryan again. I couldn't go to the light without Bryndle, and if she wasn't there, I couldn't be either. My grandmother smiled encouragingly, and I knew I had made the right decision. I watched them slowly disappear into the fading light.

I walked back toward my body, not fully understanding the gravity of my decision, the path that would unfold before me, or the truth that my soul's path had been set in motion even before I was born.

CHAPTER FOUR

What Now?

HOVERING ABOVE MY BODY, I realized my original plan wasn't going to work. I had envisioned that once my spirit was free from my body, I would be with Bryndle. She would be safe, and we would be together for eternity. Instead, I was alone, just my spirit self and my body. Doubt filled my soul as my body lay still at my feet. I felt small and helpless. That was always my problem—too often I thought only of myself and what I could or couldn't do.

Then Michael's words echoed in my mind. Why did I feel like I knew him? It seemed like his presence hovered just beyond reach. I kept trying to remember how I knew him, but I couldn't place him. He said I carried a power I did not yet understand. I couldn't comprehend what that meant—yet, for some reason, I believed him.

I have power inside me. I can do this, I repeated to myself like a mantra, again and again. *I have to. I know I can. Look at what I have already done.*

My confidence restored, even if I didn't know quite what I was doing, I resolved to figure it out, one step at a time. I acknowledged that at times during this journey I might feel unsure or frightened and that I had no idea what lay ahead. I vowed I would not doubt myself or my abilities again. Michael's words gave me hope, an assurance that what I had set out to do was possible. I also knew it was vital to let the universe know of my intent.

I can do this. I will save my Bryndle! I yelled to the surrounding forest, determined to raise positive vibrations in the outside world, as well as within myself.

The first thing I had to do was stop looking at my body. It had an almost hypnotizing effect on me. I found myself studying it, missing my life and my family. I couldn't focus on the past. I had to focus on the spiritual world where I was now and where I needed to search for Bryndle.

I called out to her, but she did not respond. As I walked around the forest clearing, I was unable to venture too far from my body. I knew that while my body lay undiscovered and uncared for, I would have one foot in the physical world and one in the spiritual world. I knew I needed to be fully in the spiritual world before I could even attempt to find Bryndle.

I felt myself becoming deeply connected to the surrounding woods, which felt a bit like home. It reminded me of my family and Bryndle in a good way. Christmas ornaments, including a photo of the two of us, hung from a nearby pine tree. Still, they reminded me of why I was still here. I needed my body to be found. I needed to be free. My body bound me to the physical world.

Please find my body, please find my body, I called throughout the night, willing the universe to deliver my message to someone, anyone.

Time passed. I heard a group of teenagers as they walked through the woods laughing and joking about a rumor that the nearby falls were haunted by the spirits of my wife and baby girl. As I listened, it saddened me to realize what deaths had caused them to come here to these now peaceful woods. I realized that my death would soon add an additional chapter to the ghost story. Stupid as it sounds, I hid behind a tree and prayed they wouldn't be the ones to find my body, but they did.

I watched them run away screaming. I realized the sight of my body was disturbing, something else I hadn't considered. I had assumed a police officer would find my body and I regretted the trauma I had caused the teens. I felt so guilty that these kids had stumbled upon the bloody scene. I could only imagine the damage I had caused their young minds. I felt even more responsible for my decision, for my violent act, and could only hope it would enable me to successfully find Bryndle. I was relieved that police officers would be coming and that my body would be well taken care of by my family.

The sound of sirens soon filled the woods and strobing red and blue lights flashed through the trees. I used to get a knot in my stomach every time I heard sirens, but this time it was different. I was excited that the sirens meant my body would be found, and I would be freed to begin my quest.

As the officers approached, I could hear them discussing that this was the area where Bryndle's horrific murder had occurred. They wondered if the murderer had struck again. Then I recognized the voice of Detective Cunningham as he ordered the officers to stay away from my body and instead to block off the area and keep the media from setting foot in the forest.

The detective then slowly approached my remains and carefully studied my body. I saw in his eyes the moment he realized it was me as he bent down to look at my left hand holding the picture of Bryndle and myself.

"Tallon," he said, his voice breaking.

Strangely, I could feel his emotion as if it were my own. He appeared heartbroken at the sight of my suicide, and I sensed his deep feelings of responsibility for my death. I had not realized how strongly he felt that he had let me down by failing to discover who had killed Bryndle and Oryan—even though I had never blamed him. As I witnessed this tough man break down and cry at the sight of my body, I cried as well with shame and guilt for the way he was affected by my suicide.

"What have you done?" he said as he stared at the photograph I was holding in my hand. "Oh, Tallon, I know you missed her, honey, but this wasn't the answer." Eventually, his tears turned to anger as he stood and kicked a tree behind him. "God damn it," he yelled, startling nearby officers.

Detective Cunningham was a good man. I came to know him well as he investigated what the press dubbed The Monroe Murders. During the past three years, he had become close to me and my family. I'd heard many stories of investigating detectives ignoring victim's families, especially years after the crime, but that wasn't my experience. Detective Cunningham called me weekly, even if it was just to say hello and ask how we were coping. I knew he was deeply affected by Bryndle's and Oryan's murders, and he had made it clear he would never give up trying to solve their case. Watching him now, I realized how much more I had added to his pain and regret for not solving the case.

Then he turned back to my body and gently pulled a piece of paper out of my pocket and unfolded it with a gloved hand.

I'm sorry. I love you all so very much, but I just want to be with Bryndle and my baby. Forgive me. Tallon.

I had put it in my pocket yesterday morning to ensure there would be no question that I had committed suicide. I needed to let everyone know why I had taken my life.

"It's Tallon Monroe. It's not a crime scene. She killed herself. Tell the coroner it's okay to take her body back to the morgue," Detective Cunningham said to the waiting officers. He stood and walked away; his shoulders slumped in defeat.

I watched the coroner's people carefully place my body inside a black plastic bag, zip the bag closed and take it away. I cried. I whispered my gratitude as I said goodbye to my body. It had been such a part of me and now we were being separated forever. Letting go was difficult as I mourned the end of my physical life.

CHAPTER FIVE

Priorities

TAKING MY LIFE WASN'T the first time I made a decision that I could never take back. My life was full of those kinds of choices—some I learned from, others filled me with guilt and regret. Trust me, sometimes our choices set in motion unforeseen outcomes. For example, the night I chose to let work become more important than being with her, my family. That night she was out alone because of my decision. I can't take it back, and it has haunted me ever since. That choice ultimately ended Bryndle's and Oryan's lives. I didn't realize then that it was just one of a series of choices I made that contributed to their deaths and to my own.

After losing them, I was different. I changed, and my priorities changed. I was still dedicated to being Director of Development for one of the nation's top-rated adolescent treatment facilities for sexual misconduct and I kept the two hundred bed facility full to the best of my ability. Yet I determined never again to allow my work to interfere with my personal life. Before I lost them, I believed my work mattered—and it did to some degree—but not like having them in my life, to having a family I absolutely loved. I once felt the kids I worked with sometimes needed me more than my family did. I was wrong. My family needed me more.

Had I known what I know now, I would have done so many things differently. Maybe I would have been able to save them and myself, and thus all of us would still be alive. But now, maybes were absolutely useless.

Ann and Michele Modtland

CHAPTER SIX

Emotions

IT'S DIFFICULT TO KNOW where to start, to describe what happened, and how I came to the decision to end my life. Nevertheless, this is how I experienced the shift in my soul.

It was just a typical Friday night in December. The snow seemed non-stop that year. Emi, my long-time best friend and I had started a tradition in middle school of watching chick flicks and ordering pizza, which we ended when Bryndle and I married. After Bryndle's death, we reinstated the tradition and added some heavy drinking in as well. In doing that, I once more made a choice that I can never take back. It's painful for me to talk about that fateful Friday night. All I know is I feel overwhelming guilt for my betrayal.

How could you have done this? My heart cried out to me after I had sex with Emi. She and I had nonchalantly joked several times before about having sex and even talked about how long it has been since either of us had been with someone. I am still not clear just when we crossed the line between joking and actually having sex. I wish I could say that I had too much to drink so that I could blame my actions on the alcohol, but that just wouldn't be true. I did it. I decided to have sex with Emi. That night I was needy and weak. I was lonely and needed to be touched. I won't lie—physically, it felt good. It had been so long since a woman had touched my body that way, since someone wanted to hold me, since someone desired me. Quite simply, I needed the physical release. After, as my breathing calmed and I regained control of my body, the reality of my choice became clear.

"Oh, my God," I said as I leapt to my feet. My necklace, the necklace that was a gift from my parents on my wedding day to Bryndle, fell to the floor as if protesting my actions. I leaned to pick it up and held it for a moment. It was beautiful, an infinity symbol covered in diamonds with our names, Bryndle and Tallon, engraved on the back. How could I have thought only of myself? What had I done?

I let out small cry, my fingers trembling as I buttoned up my red shirt. I couldn't have felt more exposed and needed to cover my nakedness. Emi had never had a problem being naked. Even when we were younger, taking off her clothes was not an issue. I remember in gym class she was confident when taking showers, while I would always try to hide in a corner, hoping that no one was looking at me. Bryndle was the only one with whom I could utterly expose myself and feel completely safe. She always made me feel attractive.

As I dressed that night in Emi's living room, I remembered how Bryndle would challenge me to games of strip poker and how I never minded when Bryndle always won and I would end up naked while Bryndle remained completely clothed, laughing. She turned everything into a game, and I had adored it. The memory always made me smile. So why didn't I think of her when I was so caught up with my own needs while having sex with Emi? I knew Bryndle would have never done that to me.

Emi just sprawled there on the couch naked, sweaty, and out of breath. I grabbed her T-shirt from the end table and threw it to her. She calmly sat up, pulling her thick brown hair into a ponytail. When I finally had my black suit pants and jacket all buttoned up, I felt put back together. I may not have always felt confident on the inside, but on the outside, I always strove to look professional and on point.

"Have you seen my shoes?" I just wanted to escape what I had done. As usual, her clothes were strewn on the floor—messy, just like the condition of the rest of her home. Her house wasn't filthy, but it was always cluttered and disorganized.

"*Relajarse*, Tallon," Emi said to me calmly in her native Spanish, slowly putting on her T-shirt as if nothing had happened.

"Relax?" I couldn't believe she said that. I had just cheated on my wife and she was telling me to relax.

"Do you realize what I have done?" I couldn't stop touching my wedding ring. It meant so much to me and was a painful reminder of my mistake.

"How could I have betrayed Bryndle like this?" I moved to put dishes in the kitchen sink. I have always been somewhat of a neat freak, but after the murders, my cleanliness had become obsessive. I guess it was my way of convincing myself I had control of something, but the truth is we never have control. When everything feels wrong or when things aren't in order, I can't breathe. At this moment, it felt like the walls were rapidly moving in all around me.

"I need to get out of here," I said to myself, not realizing I had spoken out loud again.

"We had sex, Tallon," Emi said quietly. "That's all." She slowly stood up and walked to the fridge.

Sex—I continued to twist my wedding ring. Yes, it was just sex, but I think that made it worse. For Emi, casual sex was something she accepted as normal, but for me, intimacy was important, and this frank attitude made me uncomfortable.

"Want something to drink?" Emi asked as she popped open a beer. I shook my head.

Her voice was obviously pained, but I ignored it. I had wanted the sex, but I just hadn't expected the emotional impact—although I should have if I had just connected with my true feelings.

"Tallon," Emi stepped toward me to force eye contact, "It's been three years. You didn't do anything wrong."

"It's been two years, eleven months, and nineteen days," I corrected as a tear slipped down my face. I took a deep breath to regain my composure.

"Come on, Chewy," I called to my large brown shaggy mutt of a dog, remembering anew how Bryndle and I had adopted him from the shelter shortly after we found out we were pregnant.

"Tallon, I thought we talked about this?" said Emi, obviously confused. "I thought it was what you wanted. What we wanted."

I didn't say anything. I was overwhelmed emotionally. I will always regret not taking care of Emi's heart that night. I was someone she trusted. We had just had sex and I was treating her like she didn't matter. I was only concerned about my own broken heart.

Yet, the lesson I learned that night was profound. I learned that even with Bryndle gone, she would be my one true love, and being with anyone else would be impossible. Bryndle was my wife and always would be. At our wedding, we never said until death do us part. It sounded ridiculous to us—as if love stopped when one of you died. We believed we were married for eternity and that our love would never change. The experience with Emi only confirmed that truth for me.

I can see now that, in that moment, I was completely crippled by pain. Chewy and I went back to the house. I called it the house because without Bryndle and Oryan, it just didn't feel like a home anymore. It felt empty, abandoned. I couldn't even park in the garage because the baby stroller we bought together was still sitting there. Bryndle's coat—her red, puffy down coat—still hung on the coat rack near the front door. Every time I saw it, I would think of the day we had a snowball fight in the front yard. Bryndle—with her infectious laugh and beautiful big blue eyes—had been trying to keep her long blond hair out of her face. It was also a reminder. She wasn't wearing it the night she died. I put my jacket over it, so I didn't have to see it. Her nearly completed crossword puzzle still sat on the armchair in the family room. I hadn't been able to move it because it felt too soon, even after three years.

The house was cold. Bryndle had been so hot during that last trimester that we turned the heat way down to keep her comfortable. I kept it that way. It may sound crazy, but I could tell the house missed them, too. We'd built it together and all those little touches that make a house a home came from Bryndle. She had been amazing. Without her presence, the house felt depressed and abandoned—and, just like me, the house seemed to feel unsure of what its purpose was anymore. I had never explained to the house or to Chewy what had happened or why they never came back. I knew neither one would understand, and, truly, neither did I. The house was to protect us from the outside elements. I was to protect them. The house had done its job, but I had let them down.

I took Chewy to their grave site once, right after we buried them. He sniffed around before laying on their grave, refusing to leave. I remember watching him, wondering if he somehow sensed the truth of what had really happened. He lay there for more than an hour, ignoring my pleas to come. I ended up carrying him back to the car. Later that day, he refused to eat. I held him all night, reassuring him how much we all loved him. I felt like he needed to know where they were, but I have regretted taking him to their gravesite.

Sleeping in our bed that night wasn't an option, not after what Emi and I had done. Everything had disappeared—her love, her laughter, her smell, our baby, and the home we made together, and it all happened in just one moment. I felt like the only thing I had left, that was ours, I had just given to Emi.

I stood paralyzed in the family room realizing that everywhere I looked, they were still there. The baby blanket Bryndle had been crocheting still lay in the tote next to the couch. Our family picture hung on the wall where we had put it just days before they died. I studied the picture of myself holding my beautiful Bryndle, eight months pregnant, with Chewy lying at our feet.

I couldn't bear to look around my house anymore. Instead, I looked out through the French doors to focus on our backyard covered in snow. I used to love snow, but now it seemed more like Mother Nature's way to hide the secrets of the world and disguise them as beautiful. I know better now—just because something appears beautiful doesn't mean that it is. And just because you can cover something up, doesn't mean it isn't there. I tried to lose myself by watching the snowfall, but my body, my soul could no longer contain the weight of my emotions and memories. Tears flowed down my cheeks, and my legs buckled.

I remained on the family room floor that night, sobbing uncontrollably with Chewy huddled at my side. It was a long time before I fell asleep, since this was the first time, I had let myself lose control and release some of my pain. I had been out of touch with myself for so long. I had avoided looking within myself for comfort because that's where the proof resided that she was really gone.

Ann and Michele Modtland

CHAPTER SEVEN

The Christmas Party

THE NEXT MORNING, I woke to my cell phone vibrating on the hardwood floor. I hate cell phones. I know they have good qualities and can be useful, but really, it's just another tool of this fast-moving world to keep us from hearing our souls and connecting face to face with one another. Too often, people have a difficult time judging what's important and what can wait until the workweek. Normally, I would have turned it off but with everything that happened yesterday with Emi, I must have forgotten.

My phone announced a text from Nia. She was Director of Admissions and for her everything was an emergency and needed immediate attention. Although I sympathized with her because I used to feel the same way about work, it also made me resent her. Losing your family puts everything into a new perspective in a way you can't explain. It was why I always left my office cell phone at work. Nia knew this and had called my personal phone.

Nia is a kind woman and every boss's dream. She is a go-getter and had texted me just to let me know an admission date was changing. The teen was coming in on Saturday instead of Sunday. It was something that didn't affect me in any way and could have waited until I arrived at work, but she felt I needed to know.

As I read the text, I thought of Emi. I called her and apologized for my behavior the previous night. I took responsibility for what I had done, explaining how our intimacy had affected me, and acknowledging my failure to understand how my reaction might affect her. After we talked, I felt a large weight had been removed from my shoulders. She was kind and understanding, and I felt so lucky to have such an amazing person as my best friend.

Later that afternoon I received two other text messages. One was from Alice, to remind me about her Christmas party that evening, and the other one was from Emi, asking to meet for appetizers and drinks after a training session with a client.

Alice is one of those amazing moms that everyone loves, and she had been a volunteer at my treatment facility for several years. A mother of three, she always had the best snacks and hosted the best parties for the kids. She made everyone feel welcome. Neighborhood kids regularly wanted to play at her house and that's the way she liked it. She was wonderful, always happy and positive. She has a big heart and was always so supportive of me, particularly after the loss of Bryndle and Oryan.

About two years after their deaths, Alice lost her son. He was just six years old at the time and of course, she was shattered. She carried a lot of unnecessary guilt, not only for her son's death but for my loss as well. The enormous gravity of our losses merely deepened our connection and we became even closer. Although she had lost her son in a different way than I lost my family and was better at resuming her life, she always assured me that it was okay for each of us to grieve in our own way. Alice now dedicates her life to helping families deal with loss.

Alice's Christmas party was actually a psychic reading. Crazy, right? I had never heard of a group reading party before, let alone a Christmas party coupled with a psychic reading. Alice had heard from a friend about an amazing local medium named Raya. The medium had brought comfort to one of Alice's friends, who also was struggling with the death of a loved one, and said she was willing to try to help Alice as well. And Alice, being the person she was, wanted to extend the potential healing experience to all those she loved. She could have had a private reading, but she wanted to offer others a similar chance to find peace.

Before the party, I reached out to my mother for her opinion on mediums. I expected skepticism, but instead she urged me to keep an open mind. There are ways to know if it's true, ways to know if the other side really exists, she said. She advised me to think of a memory I shared with someone special that had passed away, like my grandmother. She told me that to prove the reading was real, when I was alone before the reading, I should talk out loud to my grandmother just like I did when she was alive, explain my intention, relay the memory to her and ask her to tell the medium about that memory.

I was stunned to hear my mother's advice. Her suggestion made more sense when I learned that shortly after my grandma had passed, my mother and her sister, Aunt Sally, went to see a medium. I might never have known that had I not been invited to Alice's Christmas party. Before their reading, they asked my grandmother to bring up a memory during the reading to let them know she was really there. It had worked.

I took my mother's advice and, while driving to Alice's house, I spoke out loud to my grandmother as if she were there. I talked about how we would do odd jobs around the house to earn gold coins and that the neatest thing about the coins was that they could only be used for things money couldn't buy. For example, we could use the gold coins to buy time with my grandma doing something special, like reading a book or watching the sunrise. After the quality time we spent with one another, we would put the coin in an envelope and write the date, time, and a description of the special thing we had done together and drop it in her special memory chest. My mother has that chest now, and I love to go through it and look at all the coins of past memories.

Alice's home was big, beautiful, and warm. It was decorated from top to bottom with fragrant Christmas candles and garlands. Her front room was filled with mismatched chairs squeezed between the couches and recliners, forming a semi-circle for the reading. Despite the welcoming atmosphere, I felt uncomfortable. I couldn't help but wonder if the woman I was about to meet was a fraud, making money off people's heartache.

Unfamiliar faces filled the room and white candles glowed on the coffee and end tables. The energy felt reverent, but I think most people felt the way I did, unsure about the whole thing. Then Raya entered the room. Whatever I thought a psychic medium would look like, it wasn't Raya. She walked into the room with a kind smile, confident and sure of herself, well dressed, and obviously physically fit. She looked like someone I would have done business with.

Raya began by thanking all of us for being there and for allowing her to connect with our loved ones. Next, she bowed her head, said a prayer, and asked that all messages to be received that night would be for the highest good. Although I fought to retain my skepticism, from the moment Raya spoke I could feel she had a beautiful soul and radiated love. What happened next was amazing and was both one of the best and worst experiences of my physical life.

Raya walked about the room until something, or someone, caught her attention. "I have a young boy coming through. I think he's connected to someone on this side of the room," she said as she stopped directly in front of Alice.

"It's an A name, maybe Alex or Allen? It feels like this soul is connected to someone in this area. He is showing me a motherly attachment and lots of love. Have you lost someone young?" she asked Alice. "Is this soul connected to you, or your son, perhaps?"

"Yes, I believe so." Alice's voice cracked, overcome with emotion. "My son's name is Allen."

Raya paused; head tilted as though listening to someone talking softly into her ear. "Okay, he's showing me that he passed away in water. He's showing me that his lungs are filling up with water. That is usually my sign for someone drowning."

I remember thinking everyone knew because it was in the newspaper, and a part of me wanted to protect Alice from this fraud.

"He has a great personality. He likes to tease you," she said next as her smile turned more serious. "He says you blame yourself for not locking the gate."

"He drowned in our swimming pool." Alice lowered her head. "I didn't lock the gate. It was my fault."

"He's telling me that you did lock the gate, and that he unlocked it. He keeps saying again and again that it's not your fault, and that he was always doing things he wasn't supposed to do. He says he looked at life as an adventure and is concerned that you keep replaying this horrible image of him drowning in your head. He says it's wrong, that it's not how it happened."

"Does that make sense to you?" Raya asked Alice. "He wants you to know that it was just his time. That he was in the pool, and then he was with grandpa. He's telling you that he wasn't afraid and that it didn't hurt. He's saying that you have kept the pool closed since he passed and he would like you to reopen it, that his brothers need to know he is fine and that it's okay for them to swim."

Alice nodded her head as tears dampened her face.

Raya smiled. "I like this kid. He wants you to tell his brother, Aden, that he hid his baseball cards in the garage under Dad's bowling ball because Aden wouldn't let him play with them."

Raya, Alice, and the entire room chuckled, tearful smiles on their faces.

I watched as Alice realized she was truly receiving a message from her beloved son and I saw her whole soul become lighter. I felt honored to have witnessed that. The moment felt sacred, and it was beautiful to watch as she finally released all her unnecessary guilt and fear.

Messages like that continued throughout the night. A gentleman's son, who had committed suicide, came through and gave his father peace. A woman who had lost her husband in Iraq, heard a loving message from him. People were receiving beautiful messages that their loved ones were fine and watching over them. The energy in that room was peaceful and full of love.

Raya walked in my direction. "I have a woman with a strong presence here, a grandmother or aunt coming through. Her name is Viv or Vicky. Is this for you?" she asked me.

I wasn't sure. "My grandmother's name was Vivian." What happened next validated all the events that had transpired that night.

"She's coming forward holding a gold coin," Raya said.

My mouth dropped open in surprise.

"Does that make sense to you? I'm not sure what the gold coin represents," Raya confided in confusion.

"Yes," I answered.

"She says you have her secret chocolate-chip cookie recipe." I smiled. "Yes."

"Your grandmother is bringing through some other loved ones, a couple. Are they your parents?" Raya asked.

"No, my parents are alive," I said.

"Could they be your in-laws? Okay, yes, they are confirming that they are your in-laws."

I was stunned. I had never imagined that I would hear from them.

"They want me to thank you for giving their daughter a family and a home. They are showing me a lot of love for you." Raya smiled.

"Your grandmother is holding a baby and your in-laws are surrounding her. This usually symbolizes that they are all connected as a family." Looking at me, she inquired softly. "You never got to meet or see this baby?"

Tears filled my eyes as Raya continued. "They are telling me how beautiful she is and how much they enjoy her little spirit. Oh, I can see her, and she is adorable. She has these big blue eyes and dark-brown hair just like yours," She paused for a brief moment. "This baby was never born?"

"No." I shook my head and tried to fight back the tears, but I sobbed helplessly.

"She's cute as a button. She knows she was named by someone special. Maybe an uncle? She loves her name, Oryan, which is a beautiful name by the way."

"Thank you, my brother named her, after his favorite robot hero." I couldn't help but think, where is Bryndle? Deep down, intuitively, I felt that something wasn't right. Where is Bryndle? Why wouldn't she be with our baby and her parents?

"They are telling me that someone is missing."

I shook my head, confused.

"Not missing from us, but missing from them," Raya clarified. "Your wife, has she passed as well?"

I saw Raya becoming visibly upset and emotional.

"Oh, my God," she said, her hand lifting to her chest as her voice quivered with emotion. "They are telling me she was murdered while she was pregnant."

I couldn't speak. I just nodded my head as gasps filled the room.

Bryndle come to me, please tell me you love me, that you're okay, and that you forgive me. The words I so desperately wanted to hear just weren't coming.

"Your wife, Brandy?"

"Bryndle," I corrected her.

"Okay, thank you. I knew I didn't have it exactly right. Your wife, Bryndle, she was pregnant with Oryan when she was murdered. She was pretty far along too, is that correct?" Raya asked as her eyes welled with tears.

"She would have been born in two weeks."

A tear rolled down Raya's cheek, and I noticed her husband take a couple steps toward her to see if she was okay. Raya lifted her hand and motioned for him to stop.

"Hold on for a moment, please. I am calling in more help from the spirit world, so I have a clear understanding of what's going on."

The room was silent. Raya knelt in front of me and held my hand. "This was a brutal murder. I see fire?"

I nodded.

"They are showing me that it is still unresolved, that you know she isn't with them."

Raya talked to me as if we were the only two people in the room. I couldn't speak. I was so confused by what she was saying.

"Hold on. Let me try to reach Bryndle," she said as she looked away and closed her eyes. In a moment, she turned back to me, her eyes conveying the importance of her message.

"This is sensitive and may be hard for you to hear and comprehend. Your grandmother keeps telling me you need to know. I have never experienced this situation." Raya took a deep breath. "Do you want me to continue, or would you rather continue in some place more private?"

I could tell by the way she looked at me that it was something big.

"Please, just continue," I insisted, anxious and worried by all I was hearing.

"Tallon, is that your name?"

"Yes, that's my name."

"You are Tallon?" she asked again.

I nodded. "Yes, I am Tallon."

"Okay," she said and turned to address the group. "Can I have some privacy with Tallon, please?"

Alice stood up. "Absolutely, let's all go downstairs to the game room."

With no disagreement, everyone stood and followed Alice out of the room. As the room cleared, Raya's husband approached her.

"Are you okay, babe, do you want me to stay?" he asked, touching her arm with concern.

"Yes, thank you." She gave him a small kiss, and I watched as he returned to a corner of the room. Raya pulled a chair around to sit directly in front of me.

"I am unable to reach Bryndle. Your family is telling me that they can't reach her either. Your grandma, Bryndle's parents, and your baby keep trying, but they can't reach her. Bryndle's energy is hyper-focused on the moments leading to her death. She is still trying to fight for her baby's life and doesn't know they are dead. She is still fighting, believing she must save the baby. That is all she can focus on."

"Wait, what are you saying?"

"They are telling me that you have always felt she wasn't at peace, and that you have never felt her presence around you. Is that correct?"

"Yes."

"I'm so sorry to have to give you this message, but there must be a reason for it. I trust the spirits and must be truthful. I feel like you want me to be honest." Raya reached to hold my hand.

"Yes, I do. But I just don't understand."

"Honey, Bryndle believes she is still being attacked by the murderer and is desperately trying to save the baby. That's all she can focus on, saving the baby. Sometimes, when deaths are traumatic and quick, our souls get confused and get lost. She didn't see the light when it came for them, she can't see or hear your grandma, her parents, or Oryan. She's stuck, connected to the residual energy of her death, not understanding that it's over. She is essentially living out this horrible experience again and again...believing that if she keeps fighting, she has a chance to save the baby and herself. She doesn't understand they are already dead, that she needs to move on," Raya said, her eyes filled with worry.

I was devastated. I thought hearing that your wife and your unborn child were murdered would be the worst thing one could ever hear. Now, hearing that my wife was stuck, and that she believed she was fighting for our baby's life, fighting off her attacker, was worse by far. The reality was that Bryndle was in pain, terrified, and reliving the same event repeatedly.

Horrified, I ran out the front door to the curb and vomited. I couldn't hear. I couldn't see. I was consumed with the image of Bryndle fighting for our baby not knowing they were already dead. She was stuck in an unimaginable hell. Raya was right. I had never felt Bryndle around me. I always had this unsettled feeling in my soul where she was concerned. I could sometimes feel our little baby's soul when I was in her room, and it always brought me peace. Nevertheless, I felt emptiness when it came to Bryndle. I remembered once asking my mom if she thought Bryndle still loved me because it felt like she had just disappeared and took her love with her. I carried so much guilt because I assumed Bryndle blamed me for the murder.

The voices of approaching carolers brought me back to the moment. Raya walked up and sat by my side on the curb. "I am so sorry that this is happening, and I can't imagine how you feel. I have never experienced anything like this before. I have asked for angels to help Bryndle. Please know that Bryndle is not alone. It is her divine right to have help. Your grandma, Oryan, and her parents continue trying to reach her, and of course her spirit guides never leave her side. They will continue to stay until they can reach her. Sometimes these things just take time."

"How could this happen? What happened to God greeting you? How could he have allowed this to happen?" I was angry.

"Well, God didn't do this, Tallon," Raya said softly. "Bryndle has to work through this. No one can do it for her."

"I know Bryndle. It's been three years, and if she believes she's fighting for our baby, she will never stop." Heartbroken, I got up and walked to my car, helpless in my despair.

CHAPTER EIGHT

Ghost Hunting

SITTING IN MY CAR as the heater struggled against the outside cold, I knew I had to figure out for myself what was happening. I thought of telling Emi, but I knew she wouldn't understand. Plus, she had recently lost her dad and I didn't want to upset her. I took out my phone and texted her that I was sorry, but I wouldn't be able to have appetizers with her that night. I was just too tired. That done, I drove around, trying to make sense of the information I had just received and to decide what to do about it. I had to know if this was true. Although I knew my grandma wouldn't lie, Raya might not have understood everything correctly. I had to know for myself.

I had watched a few ghost hunting shows on television and wondered if I could do one myself. If I could do my own mini-ghost hunt where Bryndle and Oryan were murdered, I might be able to see if Bryndle was really stuck there. If she was, I could talk to her and let her know everything was okay. I know she loved and trusted me. if I could just reach her, she would believe me. I drove to the local electronics store and purchased a digital voice recorder, a camera, a flashlight, and batteries. Next, I headed to the clearing in the forest.

I stood at the edge of the forest for a moment, fearful of what I might find. I had never stepped foot on this ground without her. We used to come to the falls every summer but after their deaths, I couldn't even look in this direction, despite its beauty. However, I knew from television coverage exactly where their bodies were found. The days after their bodies were discovered, people began leaving gifts under the pine tree where they had been left to die. I couldn't believe the outpouring of love from my friends, neighbors, and even complete strangers.

During those first few days, their televised thoughtfulness helped me feel not so alone. I felt comforted knowing people were aware of what had happened and that they cared and grieved for Bryndle and Oryan, too. They turned a horrific crime scene into a place of love and support. That following summer, a fundraising drive by the local girl scout troop raised money to place a beautiful marble bench near the falls, in memory of my wife and baby girl. I had never seen it in person, only in pictures.

I got out of my car, took a deep breath and headed into the dark woods. The smell of pine permeated the forest. These pine trees were large and old and I'm sure they had many secrets to tell. Snow lay heavy on their boughs, but that's not all they were carrying. I could feel it. They knew that unspeakable things had happened here. They were, in fact, the only witnesses to the crime.

I could hear the river, so I knew I was close. I took a deep breath and followed the river to the falls. They were typically frozen this time of the year, but I saw water and life still running under the ice where I shone my flashlight. There was a large boulder under the pine tree where my beloved was found. I was surprised to see there were still remnants of what people had left behind. I knew my dad came here from time to time to leave flowers. My parents loved Bryndle as if she were their own. Under about an inch of snow, I saw a pink bear that looked newer than the rest. I picked it up and shook off the snow. A little card was attached to its neck. *For Oryan, Love, Aunt Emi.*

I was in shock. I didn't know Emi ever came here to pay her respects, or that she really thought about Oryan and Bryndle that much. She never talked about them but would always listen when I needed to talk. I lovingly placed the bear back down next to the boulder, and it was then that I saw the bench for the first time. I walked to it. It was beautiful. In the middle of the bench was a bronze plaque with a ceramic photo of Bryndle, pregnant and in front of my parent's Christmas tree. I loved that photo of her. She looked radiant. I knew they must have gotten the photo from my mom. Under the photo were the words: *In memory of Bryndle and Oryan, may you be safe in God's arms until we meet again.*

I was so moved I could barely breathe. At the end of the bench sat a stone angel, looking down at the spot where their bodies were found. It looked so heartbroken and lonely. I knew immediately that I should have come sooner to see this beautiful display of love from the community.

I walked back to the boulder, cleared it of snow, and set the digital voice recorder down to pull out my camera and take some pictures. The whole while, I talked to Bryndle. I can't remember exactly what I said, but I know I kept telling her how much I loved her, that I missed her so much, and that I was sorry I wasn't there that night to protect her. I was emotional. I hadn't talked to her in a long time.

Occasionally, I would go to the cemetery and leave a CD of music I knew she would enjoy, or I would leave shoes for Oryan. I know it was ridiculous, but I missed them and thought of them all the time. Nevertheless, I had never really talked to her out loud, never conveyed to her how much I missed her until that night. It was difficult to articulate my emotions. I cried more than anything.

The night was quiet and lonely. I didn't see or hear anything, and I wondered if I was foolish to try to conduct my own ghost hunt. I packed up my gear and headed back to my car. My parents were expecting me. They had Chewy and had asked me if I would stay with them for a few days during my Christmas vacation. After all, it was tradition. My parents worked hard to keep us close.

As I drove to my parent's house, memories flooded my mind. Bryndle and I used to sleep there on Christmas every year. The last year we were together as a family, Chewy was only a year old, and it was our first Christmas with him. My parents' house was filled with an extra bit of excitement. They loved Chewy and we were expecting Oryan in a few weeks. She was going to be their first grandchild. It was an epic year as we played Santa Paws for Chewy and Santa Claus for Odin and our soon-to-be Oryan. We bought Chewy so many toys, bones, and treats, and we wrapped so many gifts for Oryan and Odin. Honestly, they all had more toys than they would be able to play with for years. It was ridiculous, but we were just so excited, we couldn't help it. I am so grateful that we got to have that one exceptional Christmas experience all together.

After that year, it was never the same again. Although I must say that from that special year, Chewy learned what Christmas was about. As soon as my mother put up the Christmas tree, he got excited, and if you even mentioned Santa Paws, he jumped in circles and spun around. It was just too cute.

Those memories of our last Christmas with one another always put a smile on my face. At the same time, it stung so badly, knowing that we would never be together like that again.

Ann and Michele Modtland

CHAPTER NINE

Her Voice

IT WAS ABOUT THREE in the morning by the time I arrived at my parents' house, so I was surprised to see the kitchen light still on. It had been an overwhelming night, but it still wasn't over. As I walked into the kitchen, they were all sitting at the table, the smell of my grandma's cookies filling the air. It appeared they had been making them for hours because they had several plates full of them scattered throughout the kitchen. They seemed anxious.

"Baking for the neighbors at this hour, are we?" I inquired.

"Hi, sweetheart. I am so glad you're home. Please join us. Your father and I want to talk to you," my mother said.

I sat at the table next to my father, alarmed at the concern in my mother's voice.

"Your father and I went to sleep at ten, as usual, but we were awakened by a disturbing dream about you. We are so worried about you, sweetheart."

She wouldn't go into a lot of detail but said that at the end of the dream my grandmother came to her holding a gold coin. As she placed the gold coin in my mother's hand, she told my mother that I was on a path she wouldn't be able to understand. She also assured my mother that although the path I was about to embark on would be a test of emotional strength and character, I would be fine and not to worry about me.

"I couldn't go back to sleep without seeing you, without making sure you were all right. Are you okay, Tallon? You know how much we love you, right?" My mom said, sounding desperate.

I nodded and continued to listen. I just sat there and didn't say anything. Where would I even begin?

"As we were waiting for you, I had a strong urge to bake your grandmother's cookies. I know they are your favorite," my mother said anxiously.

"Thank you," I whispered.

I sat there dumbfounded. Everything seemed to be so connected. It took me by surprise. What did my grandma mean about my path? I was on emotional overload and my parents seemed to sense it.

My father spoke up finally. "If you don't want to talk tonight, honey, it can wait. We just needed to see you, to know that you are okay before we could try to go back to sleep."

Let me tell you a little about my parents, Arthur and Rose. I won the lottery when it came to parents. They were high school sweethearts and had me when they were only eighteen. They must have been wise beyond their years because I see other eighteen-year-olds having babies and they just don't have it down. My parents did. I can remember my dad working during the day when I was very young and watching him study at the kitchen table at night. He is a clinical family psychologist, and when I was seventeen, he moved his office home so he could help with my brother, Odin. That decision, although good for my brother, proved to be annoying at times for me, especially when I was just trying to get through my college years without parental interruption. But to be honest, he always taught me to look deeper into my feelings and was a strong influence on my emotional makeup.

My mother is just as amazing. She has a twin sister named Sally. They aren't identical, but they supposedly look very much alike and people still get them confused. I never understood that, because to me they look completely different. My mom has consistently been loving and supportive. I have always known that my parents were on my side, no matter what. She cherished her children and loved being a family. My mom had a difficult time getting and staying pregnant. I remember when I was maybe five, I woke up to the sound of my mother weeping this deep painful cry in the bathroom. I ran to check on her, and I saw my dad holding her. He explained to me that mommy had a baby in her tummy and that the baby had passed away. After that first time, I never had to be told again what was happening.

I was seventeen when they had Odin, my little brother, and he became my whole world. He was born with physical and mental disabilities, but from day one he was full of sunshine and joy. Although we are close, he absolutely adored Bryndle. He was only five when Bryndle and I got married. At that time, his favorite thing to do was to be a puppy. He would crawl around nonstop and carry things in his mouth and drink out of a water bowl. We all played along, but Bryndle always took it a step further and made my brother feel special. Odin was twelve when the murder occurred. He still doesn't know how they died. We felt it was best to keep him from the pain of knowing. He believes they are in heaven watching out for him.

I have never heard my parents complain about Odin's condition. They love him and have done an amazing job as parents. My mom is homeschooling him because she feels that our school district just throws all the kids with disabilities in the same class, not even looking at their individual strengths and abilities. Like any good parent in this situation, they have used every available spot in their home to accommodate Odin's growing body and needs.

Odin loves robots and action figures, especially the ones that transform. He knows everything about them and could talk to you for days about the importance of each character. The joy they bring him is indescribable.

Sitting at the kitchen table that night with my loving parents, I shared emotions that I had never revealed to anyone before. I explained to them how I just didn't feel whole without my family. I confided to them that when Bryndle's scent faded from the house, I ordered sixteen boxes of her lotion, just so I could smell her. To my dismay, her lotion didn't smell the same on me as it did on her, so I began putting it on the furniture and on my clothes—anything to have the house smell like her. I knew it was ridiculous, but I even told them how I had bought some shoes for Oryan the week before and set them on their grave. With shame, I told them how lonely I was and how I almost had an emotional breakdown after being with Emi and realizing that Bryndle is still my wife and always will be. Death had changed nothing, and time wouldn't change that.

They just listened as I described the pain in my heart. My father held me in his arms, and my mother lovingly wiped away my tears. They honored my emotions and didn't make me feel stupid for any of my actions. Their reaction validated my need to listen to my own heart and that no one could tell me how I should feel. They kissed me good night and told me how much they loved me.

That night, I released so much emotion that the core of my spirit spoke to me again. Emotionally drained, I fell asleep on the couch in my clothes. Around five, I woke up from a nightmare. I had dreamed Bryndle was in the forest calling for me. In a panic, I leapt to my feet, realizing I had to know if this was true, if she was really stuck in her own nightmare. I wondered if maybe I had captured something in my ghost hunt. I pulled out the digital voice recorder and camera and listened as I flipped through the pictures. Then it happened and everything I believed changed in that short moment. My heart stopped as I heard her voice.

Help! Please help my baby. Please.

The sound of her disembodied voice coming from the recorder as she screamed and begged for help stunned me. An hour before this experience, I would have given anything to hear her voice again. But now, hearing the pain in her voice, I was in absolute terror. A few more minutes into the recording I again heard her call out for me in a desperate, heartbreaking cry—*Tallon!* I wept. I set the pictures to the side as I focused on listening to the recorder, searching for her voice, for a clue as to what to do. I was emotionally distraught listening to her calling to me for help.

As the sun finally rose, my first impulse was to call Emi. I snuck out the kitchen door with my cell phone. I explained the events of the previous night and what I had heard on the digital voice recorder, expecting her reaction to be just as emotionally involved as mine. I was expecting her support in helping me solve this problem, but that wasn't what I got. To my surprise, she became furious. She accused me of chasing ghosts as an excuse not to move on. She claimed that I knew Bryndle was okay and that I just wanted attention.

Even though I was shocked to be accused, this way by my best friend so I strove to remain calm. "Emi, how could you possibly understand what I am going through, you've never been in a serious relationship," I said and hung up. I should have known that Emi couldn't have understood. Not only had she never had a serious relationship, she wasn't good in situations that made her feel uncomfortable. Then I realized I was just fooling myself. I really didn't have the right to talk about this to anyone. Who could possibly understand all of this? Death was scary enough and I had no right to add to others' fears with everything I was learning. The real question was how was I going to help Bryndle?

CHAPTER TEN

Winter and Ruby Boren

I DUG OUT THE card that Raya had given me that night after the party. At this point, she was really my only hope. I called and told her about what I had done after the reading and asked for her advice on the recordings I had captured. She explained the parapsychology community called the recording an EVP—an electronic voice phenomenon. She knew little about EVPs, but had a long-time friend named Winter Boren who was an EVP specialist. His wife, Ruby, had a degree in parapsychology and Raya was sure they would be happy to help me. She gave me their contact information and asked me to keep her informed about my efforts to contact Bryndle. I assured her I would.

Later that afternoon, I met Winter and Ruby Boren. They were two people who had an immediate and tremendous impact on me, as they showed compassion and honesty at a time when I needed it most. I was so grateful to have crossed paths with these kind, soft hearted, authentic people. Winter was a tall muscular man with beautiful dark skin and soulful eyes. Ruby was gorgeous—smaller in stature, of Jewish descent and she positively oozed love. In the eyes of the world, the Borens would be described as an attractive couple, but their beauty was more than superficial—it was trustworthy and shone from their souls. Ruby was soft-spoken and kind, and it was obvious she adored her husband. I found Winter to be guarded at first, but as I got to know him, it became apparent that Ruby's influence had an ability to reveal his kind and gentle heart. Together they shared a beautiful connection.

They were the most open-minded, nonjudgmental people I had ever met, never pushing their agenda and just wanting to help others. They gave me what information they had about EVPs and in the process allowed me to decide for myself the truth of the phenomenon. As we talked, it was clear they were more than willing to help me. Together they analyzed my EVP and Ruby looked through all my photos. I had not had a chance to go through all the pictures in my camera, but Ruby found two shots that appeared to contain an outline of Bryndle.

My heart pounded. Could this manifestation caught on camera really be my wife? In one picture, she appeared to reach toward me. Did she see me? Did she know it was me? So many questions filled my mind. In the other picture, she stood under a tree looking in my direction.

They explained to me that this could just be residual energy caught on the camera—energy that is left behind by a traumatic event. Yet, it was clear they were holding something back.

"What? What is it? Please, I need to know," I begged them.

Ruby looked at Winter and then at me. Winter reached and put his hand on hers. She was silent for a moment and then took a breath, seeming to make up her mind.

"We don't want to alarm you, and we don't know for certain yet. It's just that in most cases, these types of pictures usually pick up residual energy. But in these pictures, there are some inconsistencies that lead us to question if the images are merely residual energy," Ruby said quietly.

"I don't understand, what does...what does that mean?"

"Well, Tallon, it doesn't necessarily mean anything at this point, but this is why we are a little concerned. In the photos you took with your camera, Bryndle appears to be responding to your presence, meaning to the present time. If that is the case, it would rule out the possibility of it being residual energy and it would be more indicative of an intelligent haunt," Winter explained, as he continued to hold Ruby's hand.

"An intelligent haunt?" I covered my mouth; not sure I liked the term. "What does that mean?"

"It's hard to tell for sure without further investigation, but it looks as if she is aware of your presence. If she is, it means it's her actual soul, or spirit, whichever term you prefer, that you are seeing. And it could mean she hasn't moved on but is tied to this location for some reason."

I was silent for I don't know how long, taking in what they had told me. I realized that everything Raya had told me at the reading was true. I looked more closely at the pictures I had taken, and tears flooded my eyes.

My beautiful Bryndle's silhouette was distorted in the pictures and she didn't look quite whole. Was it because of all the burns and knife wounds her body had endured? It was a cruel reminder of what she must be enduring if she was trapped in the forest to repeatedly relive the murder. These thoughts triggered a memory from the night her body was found. I had insisted on seeing her no matter her condition. I had thought I needed to see her for closure, that I needed to know for myself what she had experienced. Yet, when they pulled back the sheet, the sheer horror of seeing her body left me frozen and speechless. The slashed and burned body was unrecognizable. How could someone do this to another human being, much less to my beautiful Bryndle and our unborn baby girl? I can't even begin to explain what I felt in a moment as traumatic as that, at the realization of all they suffered, and that I had been nowhere around to help. At first, I refused to believe it was them. Then I saw Bryndle's pinky toe still covered with the pink glitter Odin had helped her paint on as they both giggled just days before. Pink was her favorite color.

As these thoughts raged through my mind, Ruby and Winter said they wanted to do some research. That they planned to investigate further to know for sure that we were seeing Bryndle's soul and not just a reflection of a long-ago tragic event. They offered to conduct a professional investigation at no charge because of the unique facts of the case.

"Yes, please, how soon can you do it?" I blurted. I was desperate and needed answers.

Winter and Ruby looked at one another, and Winter nodded agreement. "With tonight being December twenty-third, so close to Christmas, the spiritual energy will be high. It will probably be a great night to do some further investigation. We understand your concern and need for immediate answers. I would want them, too," Ruby said.

"Oh, my gosh, that is perfect, thank you so much! What time should we meet?" I said with eagerness in my voice.

Winter glanced quickly at Ruby and then turned to me. "Tallon, it would be best if we conduct the investigation alone. I know this must be hard to hear, but it is important to get accurate results. I'm worried your emotions might prevent the investigation from being completely objective."

I was crushed. I just wanted to be with Bryndle again. I couldn't help but feel that if she was reacting to my presence the other night, then my place was there, in the forest, with her. Desperate for answers and knowing that I had few options, I mumbled an agreement.

Recognizing I was disappointed and upset, they tried to make me feel part of the process. Winter and Ruby spent hours together, and individually, talking to me about how they would conduct the investigation that evening. They explained the significance and limits of EVP, of how such phenomena were tested and verified. They showed me studies and examples of residual energy and how to tell them apart from intelligent haunts. They explained how special dates relevant to the deceased seem to increase a spirit's ability to communicate. For example, Ruby lost her mother a few years back but could communicate with her every year on her birthday and on Hanukah, due to the significance of these dates in her mother's life.

"Even spirits that go to the light can travel back to this realm, usually to places that were important to them during their lifetimes," Ruby explained. "And the interesting thing is that they seem to do so more frequently on dates that hold personal significance—birthdays, holidays, or the anniversary of a loved one's death. Sometimes they randomly check on a living loved one who is struggling with the death. Although this seems to be the norm for most spirits, in cases of an unforeseen or highly traumatic event, such as a murder, suicide, or an unexpected sudden accident, the souls remain stuck between the physical and spiritual worlds, unable to come back and unable to pass beyond. These types of deaths usually cause great confusion for the souls involved. For example, they might not realize they are dead, they might be afraid to move on, to go to the light, or to leave their loved ones, keeping them earth-bound and forever tethered to the place where their death happened."

Ruby's words hit home hard and the thought of that possibly happening to Bryndle crippled me emotionally. I had to help my beloved Bryndle escape the horror of her death and find the light. Whatever it took, whatever I had to do.

The following morning, Christmas Eve morning, I met Ruby and Winter at a local diner to examine the results of their investigation. It was relatively quiet there that morning and we settled into a booth at the back of the coffee shop. I offered to buy Winter and Ruby a coffee and a Danish, but they declined. Ruby slid her laptop to a spot on the table where we all could see the findings.

"Well, let's just dive into this, shall we?" Ruby said.

"Please," I said, my voice shaking with both desperation and anticipation.

They were thorough as they revealed the findings of their investigation into Bryndle's spirit status and helped me understand the implications. They captured several images of Bryndle and showed me several other images that appeared to capture Bryndle's energy signature. Winter pointed out that her injuries were present in all the pictures and seemed to progress with each image—something they had never before encountered in an investigation.

"This, Tallon, is plausible evidence that Bryndle seems to be reliving the events of the murder in real time each night," Winter said.

"Meaning that it's most likely residual energy, not Bryndle actually reliving the murder again and again, right?" I asked, praying that my analysis was correct.

"That's what we thought at first, too," Winter said. "But then Ruby was able to capture several EVPs of Bryndle trying to communicate— short EVPs, mainly just a word or two. She interacted with us in real time, trying to communicate and ask us for help. Her voice was desperate, begging us to help save her baby's life."

"We also tried to reach Bryndle through the spirit box," Ruby added.

I had never heard of a spirit box. It was a phrase from a world foreign to me. Winter explained that the box was just a radio that has been modified to sweep through AM/FM frequencies at a high rate. The sweeps apparently provide spirits an opportunity to manipulate sounds into words, giving them yet another way to communicate.

"The only time we received a response from Bryndle using this device was when we mentioned your name," Ruby said. "We told Bryndle we were friends of yours and that you had sent us to help her. Bryndle responded through the spirit box with an emotional *Tallon, help me!* and *Where is Tallon?*"

I could tell Ruby and Winter were just as distraught as I by their findings. As Winter played a few of the EVPs for me, the sound of Bryndle's voice begging for help shook me to my core. It is devastating to realize that the woman you love needs you, and that you have been letting her down for years.

I felt dizzy, knowing she was calling for me and asking for my help. I should have been there. None of this should have happened, but it did. There was no doubt. My beloved wife truly believed she was still fighting for not only her own life, but our baby's life. She just couldn't accept that they were dead, that it was over. I was desperate to help her.

"What do I do now? She's been enduring this for more than three years!" I cried out as I grabbed a napkin from the dispenser to wipe my eyes. All I wanted was to know what I could do to help Bryndle.

"Winter and I have already contacted Raya to update her on everything. Raya is really struggling with the fact that she was asked to deliver such a difficult message to you from the spirit world. She wants to help in any way possible. You need to understand that she feels this is out of her realm of expertise as she has never had a situation like this before. To get some guidance, she has reached out to her spiritual mentor, Delores, who suggested we could perform a prayer circle for Bryndle in the forest tomorrow, Christmas day, which is a high spiritual energy day," Ruby suggested.

"The prayer circle is scheduled for seven tomorrow night," Winter said.

"That is, if you are comfortable with this," Ruby added. "A prayer circle can include anyone you would like to invite, but the more spiritual leaders who understand the power of spiritual energy and the more loved ones who are closest to Bryndle that can be involved, the more powerful and successful a prayer circle tends to be.

"Raya and Delores are willing to lead the prayer circle, and they can invite a few more spiritual leaders they personally know, if you approve. We will gather everyone, including you and whoever you invite, in a circle where we will all hold hands, bow our heads and close our eyes while we imagine Bryndle surrounded in love and light. The intention is to make Bryndle feel safe by surrounding her with a collective energy created in love from those closest to her, and others who feel love toward her. Within the safety of that light, the hope is we can help her to not only see, but to walk into the light. A collective intention is a centuries-old spiritual practice that is believed to be powerful in helping those in need. By collectively sending her positive energy in the form of love and light, we may be able to raise the spiritual energy vibration around her and give her an opportunity to see past her fear. Raya's hope is that once she sees the light her parents, your grandmother, and Oryan will finally be able to reach her and help convince her of the importance of walking into the light."

Winter, Ruby, and I decided to hold a candlelight vigil, as well. They suggested that it would be a good idea to contact Bryndle's family priest to participate. They also thought it would be a good idea to invite a shaman with a strong spiritual connection to the earth to bless the land before we held these spiritual services.

After our meeting, I decided to contact Detective Cunningham to see if he could help me organize the candlelight vigil. During the years, he had truly become a dear friend. He was more than willing to do a press release that afternoon to ask the community to join in honoring the memories of Bryndle and Oryan in the forest by the falls. I found myself choking up at how he ended the press release.

Christmas is the perfect day for our community to show respect by performing a candlelight vigil and to let the act serve as a reminder that we will never forget these valued members of our community, Bryndle Monroe and her unborn child, Oryan.

I was aware that the odds of anyone showing up at seven on Christmas evening would be slim, but I had to try. My Bryndle was enduring an eternal hell, and I was determined to do everything I could to possibly help her.

Ann and Michele Modtland

CHAPTER ELEVEN

Love and Light

ON CHRISTMAS DAY, MY family, Detective Cunningham and I arrived in the forest around six. My mom had suggested that we decorate the pine tree closest to the memorial bench to help set the tone for the evening. We spent most of that afternoon shopping for ornaments, white candles, flowers, and stuffed baby animals in honor of Oryan. It was a difficult task to accomplish on a holiday. Although my family and Detective Cunningham knew this was important to me, they had no idea what my true motives were.

How do you even go about putting more worry and concern on your loved ones? Of them knowing the hell Bryndle was enduring night after night? And to be honest, after Emi's reaction, I had no idea who would even believe me. Nevertheless, having their love and support that evening meant the world to me.

We decorated the pine tree as far up as we could reach. It looked beautiful and festive. My brother Odin even brought a few of his favorite robot action figures that he wanted to leave under the tree as gifts.

"Buddy, you don't have to do that. I know how much your toys mean to you and some of these are the ones you just got this morning from Santa Claus. Just having you here will mean so much to Bryndle and Oryan," I said as I started gathering up the toys he had placed under the tree.

That angered Odin and he grabbed the toys out of my arms. "But Tallon, I'm Uncle Odin, and I promised to share my toys with Oryan. She doesn't have any. And Bryndle will love to play with Oryan just like she used to play with me. They are my favorite presents to share with my family. I want Bryndle and Oryan to have fun, too. I love them, Tallon," he said, voice cracking as he tried not to cry.

As I watched him fight his feelings of betrayal, I knew I had done the wrong thing. I knew we all show our love in different ways, and this was the most meaningful way Odin knew how to share his love. Touched by his caring, all I could do was pat him on his shoulder and comfort him. "Okay, buddy, okay."

Odin carefully placed his toys back under the tree, and I mentally made note of what each one looked like so that I could replace them later. I loved my brother, and in that moment, I understood his profound attachment to Bryndle, the pride he had in being Uncle Odin to our unborn child, and the significant loss he still suffered with their passing.

Around six forty-five, we heard people arriving and walked to the clearing in the forest. Winter and Ruby were the first to arrive and their presence helped me to feel more confident in the true meaning behind the spiritual traditions we were about to perform. I hugged each of them tightly and thanked them for coming. I introduced my new friends to my parents, my brother, and to Detective Cunningham. My parents and I walked back to the car to retrieve the candles from the trunk. I had shared with them my fear that no one would show up and they assured me that, even if it was just us, we would light so many candles that Bryndle and Oryan would be able to see us all the way from heaven. I smiled when I saw that Odin had put flashlights on the spokes of his wheelchair to make certain Bryndle and Oryan saw him.

We arranged the candles in a semi-circle and Winter, Ruby, and Detective Cunningham bent to light them. The Catholic priest and the shaman arrived right at seven and I accepted it was just going to be us. The sun faded, and light snow fell in large beautiful flakes. We gathered in a circle and the priest was about to say a prayer when large groups of people, all holding candles, entered the clearing. I was overcome. Then the priest offered a prayer and words of condolence, while the shaman danced and sang a prayer to bless the land around us. My father spoke and led us all in singing Bryndle's favorite hymn, 'Amazing Grace.'"

Spiritually, the whole evening was truly moving. I looked around in amazement at the community support Bryndle and Oryan and all of us had received that evening. I even saw Elliot had come with his mother. He was the bagger and cart retriever at the local retail store where we shopped. Bryndle always made sure to talk to him every time we went to the store, and he was the last person to see her on the night of the murder. As Bryndle left with her purchases, she gave Elliot some new shoes that she had bought for him. I remember her talking about this—she was disturbed by his worn shoes the last time we'd seen him, and she worried that the holes would leave his feet wet and cold in the snow. The store's security camera caught their whole interaction, the final images of her beautiful life.

I remember he was one of the first and only suspects in her murder, but I always knew it wasn't him. He had a few cognitive and physical disabilities plus he had always adored Bryndle. He called Bryndle his best friend, and I remember Detective Cunningham mentioning that even when police were questioning him. "Why would I hurt my best friend?" he'd asked.

I wanted to walk to them and say hello, but I just couldn't. I was overwhelmed emotionally. It made my heart smile to see him, and so instead, and out of respect for Bryndle, I waved to him and his mother.

Throughout the vigil and prayer circle, I noticed the shaman watching me closely. I couldn't help but watch him as well as he moved around the clearing, blessing the land. When he finished by saying a quiet blessing at the spot where her body was found, he turned to me. "You must be Tallon?"

I nodded, too emotional to speak.

"I know you are feeling helpless. Your concern for Bryndle is valid and is consuming you." He paused to take a deep breath. "I can feel what you're contemplating. It may work, Tallon, but there is no guarantee. I do sense something about you, a spiritual strength I don't find in many people. You must be careful...a choice like this will impact you not only in the physical world but in the spirit realm as well. It will only work if you are truly willing to give up everything, and if you are willing to take full responsibility for the act."

As he walked toward me, renewed tears ran down my face. He gently wiped the tears away. "Tallon, you have the ability to be unstoppable. But the way you will be unstoppable is up to you." And then he walked away.

I stood there for a few minutes absorbing his words, wondering about the meaning of this final advice. Still overcome with emotion, I wasn't sure where to go or what to do. I walked back to the prayer circle as people were dispersing and I thanked as many as I could for joining us. I then turned to Winter and Ruby, intensely curious as to what they thought.

Ruby reached out and touched my arm to offer comfort. "The prayer circle was powerful and moving. It carried an abundance of love."

"Tallon, Ruby and I feel that combined with the candlelight vigil's blessings and singing, the prayer circle created an energy that makes our chance to reach Bryndle strong. We have to give it time, but there is so much more hope now. All we can do is wait, so go enjoy the rest of the holiday. We feel confident it worked and we will be in touch in the next few days."

I thanked them both for their help and for being there. As I hugged them goodbye, I should have felt relieved at hearing their words—and I did my best to hold on to the hope they were trying to give me—but I couldn't help but acknowledge the truth I knew deep inside me.

CHAPTER TWELVE

Preparation

ON THE DAY AFTER Christmas, I met Winter and Ruby once again at the coffee shop where we sat in the same booth. I had noticed the intensity of their demeanor as soon as they arrived and immediately felt sick to my stomach.

"Tallon, we performed another investigation later that Christmas night. We expected not to find anything, except perhaps some lingering residual energy. But, that's not what happened. Our investigation found only stronger evidence of Bryndle's continuing battle."

It hurt to hear it confirmed out loud, but it was something my soul already knew.

Ruby continued. "Tallon, I'm sorry. I know this is extremely hard to hear. We wanted to deliver good news and honestly thought we would be doing that. You see, when we decided to conduct another investigation last night after the prayer circle, we thought because it was Christmas night there would be a high spiritual energy field and that it would help us know for sure that we had helped Bryndle to move on."

Ruby paused, her eyes filling with tears as she spoke those fateful and anticipated words. "Tallon, it's clear she hasn't moved on and now we are really concerned. So much love and light has been sent to her. We were so sure she would move to the light during the prayer circle. We don't really understand why she didn't."

Everything I feared, everything that my heart feared, had come true. The love of my life was in a constant struggle, reliving immense pain and fear again and again and again. I knew Bryndle's love for our baby and her determination to save that precious life was what was holding her there. She would never stop fighting for our baby. I couldn't blame her. I would do the same thing, and I think most people would, too.

"She's not ready, but one day her spirit guides and loved ones on the other side will successfully reach her," Winter said.

I wasn't sure how telling me that one day she would be free of this torment was supposed to bring me comfort. Their words became just a background hum as my mind formulated a plan. I could feel they were concerned for me and for Bryndle, and I knew they were trying their best. I did my best to let them believe that I was fine and that I knew we had tried everything possible. I thanked them for their help, and we embraced as we said goodbye. Winter and Ruby said they would keep in touch and would continue to check on Bryndle. I kept silent about my conviction that there was one more thing I could try to finally free Bryndle, to let her know she could finally stop her battle to protect our child.

And so, I began my preparations. I was obsessed with my plan and meticulous in its details. I sent an email to work announcing my resignation. I shipped my laptop back to them and told them where to find my work phone. I made sure my will was in order. I had never touched the life insurance that I had received from Bryndle's death, so I updated my will to make sure the insurance and all my assets would transfer to my parents upon my death. I packed up my belongings and I took all our precious baby items to my Aunt Sally. Her daughter, Cecilia, was expecting a baby boy in a couple of months. When Aunt Sally had previously asked for Oryan's crib, I was filled with an angry resentment. I felt like she had no right to use it, but now everything was so different. It didn't seem wrong anymore. In fact, it felt necessary that someone should use these untouched items.

The only thing I felt that wasn't settled was my relationship with Emi. I couldn't leave things the way they were. She was my life-long best friend. When I finally knocked on Emi's door, she stood there looking at me with obvious hurt in her expression. She waved me in and as I entered, I noticed that her house was clean and organized. I told Emi how great the place looked and how impressed I was.

"Well, I have decided that it's time for me to grow up," she said with a short laugh that clearly showed how uncertain she had been about my reaction.

I looked down, ashamed of what I had said to her the last time I was there. "I am so sorry, Emi," I said, drawing up my courage to be completely honest. "You are such an incredible woman and I had no right to say those things to you. You have so many amazing talents, so much to offer. You are going to make a special someone deeply happy one day. I know that with all my heart. I want you to know how much I appreciate your friendship. You are my best friend and always have been. I haven't felt right since our argument and I wanted to stop by and thank you for always being there for me. You're not just my best friend, you are part of my family. So, come here and give me a hug. I need to know everything is okay."

We stood for a long while holding one another.

"I have to go," I said, finally releasing her from the embrace. I tried not to be overly emotional and prayed she wouldn't realize that I was saying a final goodbye. We had been through so much together, and in my heart, I worried how she would manage without me. As I walked toward my car, I turned back around. Emi was standing in the doorway watching me leave.

"Oh, Emi, can you do me a favor?" I had forgotten one final item on my to-do list.

"Of course, anything."

"Odin has a big basketball game next Thursday and I will be out of town. Can you go for me and give him some support in my absence?"

She smiled and nodded. "I was already planning on being there. I love that boy. Too bad you won't be able to make it, but don't worry. I will cheer extra loud on your behalf." Emi grinned, and with that I knew she was as relieved as I was to be on good terms again.

"Thanks," I said. Then, I couldn't help but run back to give her one more tight hug. As I turned to walk back to my car, she grabbed my arm.

"Why does this feel like a goodbye, Tallon? Is everything okay?"

I forced myself to laugh lightly. "Everything is perfect, Emi. It's never goodbye between us and I will see you soon. I just realized I had never really told you how glad I am that you're my best friend. I want you to know I love you," I said, as I turned for the last time and walked away.

CHAPTER THIRTEEN

The Act

IT WAS FINALLY THE day and nearly the time. I stood where their bodies were discovered exactly three years before—on the ninth hour and thirteenth minute of the evening of the third of January. It would be nine thirteen in a few short minutes. I stared at the large pine tree with Christmas ornaments still hanging from its branches.

The gun was heavy in my hand. I positioned my cell phone on a boulder where I could watch the time. I pinned the photo of Bryndle and myself to the tree, making sure I would be able to see it right up to my final moments. This tree already held so many secrets, and it was about to hold another. I had never before contemplated suicide and it truly didn't feel like that was what I was about to do.

Justifying the necessity of my plan, I kept telling myself that this step would allow me to get to the same place as Bryndle, would allow me finally to help her. To be honest, the thought of taking my own life petrified me. I was so afraid God would never forgive me, no matter how good my intentions. I knew I was in my right mind, that I fully understood what I was about to do, and that I was making this decision regardless of its implications. I simply couldn't let Bryndle suffer even one more day. I knew my suicide would hurt my family deeply and I knew it would take every ounce of strength for me to complete this final act.

I looked at my phone—nine twelve. My hands trembled as I slowly put the gun in my mouth. It rattled lightly against my teeth. I can't describe in mere words the fear I had. The emotions were too strong. I sobbed uncontrollably and my tears dripped to the ground. The cold made my lips stick to the gun. My soul shuddered at the finality of what I was about to do. I had anticipated I would feel this way, so to combat my fear I reached into my breast pocket where I had placed another photo of the two of us. I held it in my left hand and looked from it to the larger photo of us pinned on the tree. I focused on Bryndle. Having a photo of her in my hand made me feel like she was there with me. I kept glancing down at my phone as this became the longest minute of my life. The time was coming soon. I forced my thoughts on Bryndle and my intent to save her. I believed with all my being that if I performed this act in the same place and time and with an unstoppable intent, I would be with Bryndle.

The numbers on my phone's screen changed. It was nine thirteen. This was it. I stared intensely at the photograph on the tree and held on tightly to the one in my hand. I pushed the barrel of the gun against the roof of my mouth. My hand shook uncontrollably, my mind shouted out one overwhelming thought– *I love you, Bryndle. I'm coming. I love you so much.*

I pulled the trigger.

CHAPTER FOURTEEN

Dimensional Warping

ALONE IN THE FOREST after they carried my body away, I was flooded with a mix of emotions. I felt trepidation and peace, both at the same time. I shut my eyes, took a deep breath, and allowed myself a sense of closure. The reality of my final act set in. My whole life, everything I knew my life to be, everything I had experienced in my life, the identity I had built during the years had been carried off in a body bag. It was all gone.

I felt humbled and strangely powerful. I thanked the universe that my intention and pleas had been heard. I felt connected to the powerful energy I had called out to when urging someone to come and find my body. The realization that this energy truly existed helped me to feel good about myself and reminded me I wasn't alone. My pleas had been heard.

So, I had to let go of my fear. I couldn't allow fear to impede my plan. I had made a commitment to myself, to my wife. I concentrated on letting any emotions regarding my body to escape. As I felt free from the connection to and responsibility for my body, I refocused on Bryndle. I had to find her, for she needed me.

I called out loudly for her. I walked toward the forest at the edge of the clearing. I knew detectives believed they had entered from the forest near here. I continued to call out to her, *Bryndle, where are you, babe, can you hear me?*

Suddenly, the sound of her scream broke through the forest. The echoing sound from the spirit world so strong that even birds of the physical world burst from the trees. I had never heard a scream like that, and it shook my soul. I ran back into the forest. I could hear her yelling and pleading.

Help. Someone, please help me.

Oh God, please God, help me! I must find her, I prayed in desperation.

I kept running but couldn't see anything. The sound of frantic feet stumbling through the snow came up behind me. I spun around, my eyes wide open, searching for Bryndle. I gasped. Finally, I saw her. She was about twenty feet away, repeatedly falling in the snow and scrambling back up as she fled her pursuer. Blood covered her face and dripped from her eyes and nose. I saw her pure panic as she ran past me. I tried to make eye contact, but she seemed unaware of my presence.

A fast-approaching movement caught my attention. As I looked over my shoulder, I saw a man in a dark coat and a full-face, black ski mask running after Bryndle. I couldn't tell who he was. Bryndle, obviously exhausted, fell to the snow-covered ground again. She grasped at her pregnant belly as she struggled back to her feet. She panted as she desperately cried out for help. Then, she fell again, her body going limp as she fell face-first into the snow.

Oh, my God, Bryndle get up! I screamed as I frantically ran to help her. I heard the attacker's footsteps getting closer. His build was intimidating. He was tall, muscular, and physically fit. He was about to run past me as he headed in Bryndle's direction. I leaped out to tackle him, but to my surprise, I fell right through him and onto a carpeted floor.

Confused, I jumped to my feet, shouting, *No, no, what happened? Where's Bryndle? Bryndle! Bryndle!* I called out as I ran about the room in panic. Finally, I dropped to my knees crying with frustration. I had just seen her, my beautiful Bryndle, beaten and bleeding and fighting for her life. And him, I saw him, her attacker! I had felt his determination to take her life. I tried, I tried to help and now...and now, where was I? As I looked around, wiping my tears away with the sleeve of my shirt, I got my bearings. This place was familiar and after a few seconds I realized it was my former workplace. It was some time in the past, before they had switched to hardwood floors. I was in the main conference room and there was a meeting underway. I stumbled backward as I saw myself sitting at the conference table with my leadership team. I didn't understand how or why I had gotten there. All I could do was just stand there and watch.

It appeared to be a regular morning team meeting to discuss the admission and discharge agenda. This was a waste of time. *Why am I here?* I wondered, slamming my fist against the wall. Of course, no one heard me. At that moment, a call came on the intercom alerting the team to an incident on the floor and asking for additional staff to respond. I watched as members of my team ran out to help. My mouth dropped in surprise as I watched myself leave with them.

Incidents happened from time to time, and our direct-care staff would go to help, but it was unusual for me to accompany them as I was no longer considered direct-care staff. I remembered this specific day, though. I went to help because we were short-staffed. I followed the team onto the floor. Once we were out in the hall, I could hear one of the male teachers screaming for help. I ran to follow as my past-self responded to the scream. As I arrived in the classroom, I saw that two adolescent boys were attacking one of our math teachers. I watched myself grab one of the boys and put him in a crisis prevention intervention hold we had been taught in our training.

Don't do it, it's not going to work, I tried to warn myself but, still, no one saw or heard me. The young man was able to get out of the hold and pin my other self to the ground. Watching that was hard. I remember all the commotion from this incident. In hope of changing the outcome, I reached for the young man and I fell right through him into the back seat of Detective Cunningham's squad car.

I could hear him talking on his portable radio. "It's an apparent 10-56, and the victim is identified as Tallon Monroe. I will notify the family." His head hung low and I watched him fight back tears. "Damn it," he yelled as he threw his radio at the dash.

The scene shifted again and the next thing I knew, I was watching my mother crying, harder than I had ever seen her cry.

What was happening? It was as if people's energy was pulling me to them and I was unable to control where I would be pulled next. My mother's emotions were overwhelming, and I worried she might have a heart attack. She was inconsolable. I knew this was because of me, because of what I had done. I felt so guilty having caused her this pain and prayed for my grandmother to please help comfort my parents.

"I dreamed this. I dreamed it," my mother cried out as she was held by my dad.

"All of this is just so hard to take in," my dad said, looking dazed.

"Oh, Arthur, I should have done something, maybe I could have stopped this," she said as her body shook with grief.

"I don't know how this happened, but it's not anyone's fault," my dad said softly as he kissed my mother's forehead. "Tallon has been hurting for so long. Our daughter has been hurting for so long."

My parents held one another tightly. My little brother was in the room, too, but he was just looking out the window with no emotion showing on his face. It was hard to see them hurt by the pain I caused. I went and sat by my brother, but as I turned to look at him, I found myself in Raya's kitchen.

Raya and her husband stood in front of a small television that sat on the counter. They were engrossed in a broadcast, and I soon realized they were watching the local news. The reporter was covering the story of my suicide and remarking on the fact that it was on the same date and in the same place as Bryndle's murder—when and where I had lost the love of my life and our unborn child three years earlier. Raya dropped her coffee cup to the floor. "Oh, my God, what have I done?" she cried, her hands covering her mouth. I saw the depth of her feelings of responsibility and guilt for her role in my death.

No, no, you didn't do anything. It was me. I had to do this, I called out, but she didn't acknowledge me at first. Then she slowly turned and looked in my direction. It startled me, but of course if anyone could see or hear me, it would be her. I had so much respect for Raya for telling me the truth. Some people would have hidden it from me, but she knew I had deserved to know the truth.

"Tallon, is that you?"

Yes, yes, Raya. It is. Oh, my gosh, you can hear me! I need your help.

As I answered, I felt the shift happening again as I was ripped from her kitchen to find myself in Winter and Ruby's living room. They were watching the same news report. Every time I thought I had a clear direction, I shifted to a different place. I couldn't take this anymore. This had to stop. I couldn't watch all the pain I was causing. *Please, I can't take this any longer,* I called out to the universe in frustration.

"I can't believe this," Ruby mumbled, clutching a towel as she stared intently at her television.

"She's trying to help Bryndle," Winter answered. "She has to be. I would do the same thing for you."

"I wonder if it will work?" Ruby asked, unable to turn from the television. "Tallon herself could be stuck now after committing suicide."

I listened intently to every word they said.

"It's possible, but something tells me she prepared for this," Ruby added.

"We should have seen this coming," Winter responded. "But who could have? It's nobody's fault. Let's just be here in case she needs help with anything."

He walked to the coffee table to pick up a digital voice recorder.

My heart beat faster. They understood. They knew what I was trying to do. Maybe I could communicate with them before I was pulled to another place.

"Tallon, if you can hear us, we will have a voice recorder running all the time on the coffee table. If you need help with anything, it has an alert feature on it, so we will hear it beep if you leave a message," Winter said into the air around him. He hit the record button and set the recorder back down.

Thank you, I said into the recorder. It felt good to know someone was aware I was still around and was willing to try to help me, because in that moment I felt defeated, I felt alone. As I waited for them to hear the alert that I had left a message, I thought of Bryndle again and what this all meant and how I was going to help her. Almost instantly, I found myself back in the woods.

It was dark, but flames were rising in front of me. Bryndle's howling, agonized screams filled the air. I ran toward the flames and her screams. As I got closer, I saw her body covered in fire. In desperation, she frantically rolled through the snow trying to extinguish the flames. I tried with all that I had to help her but couldn't. I could hear evil laughter as her murderer watched her burn. The flames finally extinguished, she rolled onto her back, steam rising from her body. She didn't make any more sounds and her silence was haunting. I gently lifted her head as I wept uncontrollably.

I rocked her back and forth as I tried to understand what I had just witnessed. *How could this have happened to her? How could another human being hurt her like this?* The smell of burnt flesh was overwhelming. I tried to console her by telling her I loved her. I cradled her in my arms and poured out my love for her. I noticed white light beginning to wrap around Bryndle's body and was startled when I realized it was coming from me. My hands were emitting a white light, the same light that had surrounded me when I took my own life—only this light was all a product of my love.

I held her close as I watched the light physically surround Bryndle's badly damaged body. She became engulfed in the light, and then her body disappeared. I frantically looked around, not understanding what had just happened or where she went. I looked down at my hands, and my palms were glowing. I had just witnessed my wife and unborn baby's final moments, and they were an endless hell. My pain was so great, I didn't want to exist anymore, knowing what they suffered and being unable to save them. I curled up in fetal position against the pine tree and wept, an eruption of despair from deep within my soul.

As I cried, a stillness came to me, and my mind cleared. I heard

Michael's voice in my head, reminding me. *You contain a power you do not yet understand.*

I sat up and wiped away my tears. I understood that this was just the beginning, and I needed to find that strength, that power Michael spoke of to save Bryndle. After all, it was her strength, her love, and her will that kept her fighting for our baby. That resolve, that strength was the whole reason she was trapped, and I vowed it would be my love and my will that would help her find a place of peace, regardless of what it might cost me.

With new resolve and understanding, I stood up. But as I got to my feet, I again heard her screaming and running through the snow. I ran toward her shouting.

It's okay, Bryndle I'm here. Everything is all right, Bryndle. It's over. I hoped she would hear me and stop, but she didn't. She ran past me as she did before, and as I tried to reach for her to make contact, I was pulled away.

This time, I found myself standing in our usual store's parking lot. I immediately spotted Bryndle walking to her car carrying a large grocery bag. She looked stunning. She had always been beautiful, but when she was pregnant, she somehow became even more gorgeous. As she slowly walked to Elliot, he smiled at her as he gathered carts from the cart return.

"Hey, Elliot, you know you have been so kind and helpful to me during the past few years, and I just realized I have never really thanked you," Bryndle said.

I melted at the sound of Bryndle's happy voice.

"You always thank me, Mrs. Monroe."

"Elliot, please call me Bryndle. All my friends do."

She told him this each time she saw him.

"Well, Elliot, I just want you to know how much I appreciate how you always help me get my groceries to my car and always return my cart for me. You are always so kind and thoughtful, so I got you a little gift as a thank you."

Bryndle retrieved a box from her store bag.

"Gosh, you didn't need to do that."

"It's the least I can do, Elliot. You have been a big help to me," she said, leaning forward to give him a hug.

Elliot looked in the box and grinned widely and hollered as she got into her car. "Thank you, Mrs. Monroe, um, I mean Bryndle. Gosh, these shoes are really a nice gift."

Bryndle turned and waved. "You deserve it, Elliot, you're an amazing person."

Elliot's eyes filled with tears as he watched her drive away. My heart was full. I had such an incredible wife, and it was wonderful to see her happy and alive again. I just wanted to stay in that moment a bit longer. Even so, I knew Elliot was the last person to see my wife alive, and I imagined this was the reason I was here. I needed to find out what happened next. As I ran to catch up to her car, I felt that pull again and found myself in Emi's loft.

Emi was sitting on the floor in a corner of her apartment, rocking back and forth, alone and distraught. I approached her and tried to comfort her. I sat down next to her and softly said her name. She looked up, not directly at me, but somehow sensing my presence.

I wrapped my arms around her. *What's wrong, Emi?*

A photo of the two of us fell out of her lap onto the floor. She scooped it and looked at it and then threw herself to the floor to cry even harder. We must have been eleven or twelve in that photo. My heart broke. In that moment, I knew we were in the present time—Emi had just received word I had taken my own life.

I closed my eyes and sighed deeply. I had caused so much pain to all the people I cared about. The guilt was overwhelming. There were so many people I had hurt on a profound level, but I had to keep reminding myself that if they knew the whole story they would understand. I faced Emi. I had so much love for my best friend, I knew she was hurting deeply. If the tables were turned, I would be just as heartbroken. I tried whispering to her.

I am okay, Emi, and so are you. I will always be looking out for you. I love you, Emi. You're my best friend, and you are family. Please know everything will be okay. I am so sorry for the pain I caused you.

As I said these words the white light glowed in my hands again. I closed my eyes and envisioned her surrounded in the light with love and peace. Her eyes closed and she cried out my name. She fell asleep as I lay by her side, holding her and stroking her hair.

I couldn't help but think of my actions and the profound effect they had had on the lives of the people I loved. I had to make sure my actions were not in vain. I wondered if Emi's soul could hear me. I felt a part of her was aware of my presence and that my love for her had calmed her as I held her in my arms. With that thought, I was pulled again and found myself in a hospital emergency room.

I don't understand what's going on, why am I being tossed around like this? I asked myself, feeling defeated. This had to stop. I felt so drained. It was as if I had no control of my soul. Yet, I knew there was power in the love I had for others.

I then realized numerous people were talking and I sensed a hurried energy all around me. A woman running by caught my eye. It was my mother. My heart sank as I wondered, was I in the future or the past? I walked toward her. *Mom, is everyone okay?*

She walked right through me, although she did stop for a moment and look back. I followed and saw my Aunt Sally leaning against the wall, her arms folded and her face visibly worried. As my mother approached, they embraced. I heard my mother ask about my cousin Cecilia.

"The baby is coming early. The doctor said because of all the trauma about losing Tallon, she has gone into labor and the baby is in stress. Cecilia's blood pressure is dangerously high, and they have to get the baby out. I am so worried about both of them."

Cecilia, what have I done? I thought to myself. Instantly, I found myself in her room. The atmosphere in the room was intense. I heard the doctor speak. "You're doing great, Cecilia. It's almost over, just hang on."

To my dismay, I saw her go limp. Alarms went off and a team of nurses immediately responded. I saw her soul rise to leave her body.

Cecilia, it's not your time yet, get back in your body, you can do this, I'm right here. I've got you. I closed my eyes and tried to calm and gather my energy as I spoke again to Cecilia, but this time more softly. *I'm right here. Everything is okay. You can do this.*

I opened my eyes and realized my being was glowing. I couldn't see her soul anymore. The nurses were franticly attending to Cecilia and the doctors called to prep the surgery suite for an emergency Caesarian section. It was then that I saw her eyes open as she took a deep breath.

"She's back with us," I heard a nurse alert the team.

I moved closer and she looked right at me. "Tallon," she whispered as they were placing an oxygen mask over her mouth. She kept pulling it off, trying to speak.

"Can you hear me? Can you look at me?" pleaded the nurse who was fighting with her to keep the mask on her. Cecilia wouldn't respond. She kept pointing at me, trying to say my name. "Cecilia," the nurse said again, "I need you to look at me, we are going to perform an emergency C-section. The baby is okay, but I need your full attention on me."

You've got this, honey, I reassured her. *I am right here with you.*

I held her hand as they stabilized her vitals. She calmed down, never taking her eyes off me. A few minutes later, I heard a baby's cry. Relieved that they both had made it, I watched Cecilia and her precious new baby boy as the nurses continued to monitor their progress. I followed the doctor out of the hospital room into the hall as he approached Aunt Sally and my mother.

"Baby boy and mom are both doing well," he quickly assured them. "We had a successful delivery, although we experienced a few problems. We, unfortunately, were not able to continue with the vaginal delivery, as mom was losing a lot of blood and slipping in and out of consciousness. As a result, we had to do an emergency C-section. The baby is having a little difficulty breathing on his own, which we expect at this stage. However, he is responding to oxygen and stimulation. I'm very optimistic at this point."

My aunt and my mom both sighed in relief.

"The baby will need to be closely monitored during the next few weeks," the doctor continued. "He will be in an incubator for a while to support his underdeveloped lungs. I want you to be prepared that the baby will be hooked up to all kinds of monitors and wires when you see him. Baby is being transferred to NICU where he will have twenty-four-hour care and observation. The NICU staff is incredible. He will be in the best care."

The doctor smiled as he continued to reassure them. "Mom is also doing well. However, we would like to transfer her to the ICU for the next twenty-four-hours, just so we can keep an eye on her...mainly as a precaution. I expect them both to do well. Is the father here?"

"No, my son-in-law is in the military and is currently stationed overseas. We have a call out to him to notify him of the situation," Aunt Sally explained.

The doctor nodded.

"When can we see her? I just need to see her and know she is okay," Aunt Sally asked.

"They are preparing to move her, but you can see your daughter now for just a moment."

"Thank you, doctor. Thank you for taking such good care of them both," Aunt Sally said, squeezing his hands.

I followed Aunt Sally and mother as they walked into the recovery room.

Cecilia looked pale and weak. "They took my baby to NICU. He was having a hard time breathing."

"I know, honey, the doctor told us, but he is going to be okay," Sally assured her.

Cecilia looked up at my aunt and wept. "Because of Tallon," she cried softly.

"Honey, this isn't Tallon's fault," Sally quietly explained.

"No, Mom. I mean I saw Tallon. She was here, she helped me, she saved us!" Cecilia explained, tears streaming down her face.

Saved them? I didn't save them. I caused this. *I just encouraged her not to let go,* I thought, feeling a lot of guilt. I retreated to the corner of the hospital room and thought through the events that had just occurred. How did I get to talk to Cecilia? How did she hear me and see me? As I analyzed the past few events, I realized that I had thought of Cecilia before I went into her room. I wondered if my thoughts were inadvertently connecting me with people, or whether their thoughts were connecting with me. If this was true, I wondered if I could do it again. I decided to try out my theory and focus my thoughts on Raya, because I really needed help figuring out what was going on. I needed to know why I couldn't stay in one place or time.

I closed my eyes and concentrated. It worked! I found myself in her bedroom as she was getting into bed. I spoke to her out loud, just as I had with Cecilia, but she couldn't hear me. I tried to reach for her, but I couldn't touch her in the physical world. So, I closed my eyes and tried to talk to her with my mind. Nothing worked. I even tried after she fell asleep, thinking that with her mind at rest, her consciousness might be more susceptible to hearing me. I tried all night to connect with her to no avail.

The next morning, I heard her on the phone with her mentor. Raya's eyes were brimming with tears. "I don't know how to explain it, but it's like I no longer have the ability to sense, see, or hear spirits anymore!" Raya voice was filled with anxiety as she confided in Delores. "It's like I am cut off from my abilities...maybe I am punishing myself too much, I don't know. No, you don't understand...because of me, a woman took her life. Maybe I was wrong about everything? The message I presented made someone feel hopeless and without options. I only ever wanted to bring peace with my gifts, and now I feel I no longer deserve them."

I was dismayed at the consequences of what I had done. I had hurt so many people. I was deeply worried for Raya and realized she was slipping into a dark place. I closed my eyes and focused on Raya's mentor. I didn't know Delores, but I was grateful she had come to the prayer circle. I hoped she could help me connect with Raya. I tried to connect with her through Raya's energy. It worked and I was instantly with her mentor. Delores appeared to be in her late sixties and had long gray hair. She was sitting on her front porch talking on her cell phone with a despondent Raya. She turned toward the left, in my direction.

Who are you? she asked in her mind. And I could hear her.

Surprised by her interaction with me, I answered out loud. *Tallon, Tallon Monroe.* I knew she could feel my excitement.

"Raya, can I call you back, sweetie? I will call you shortly," she said, gently setting her cell down on the table next to her.

"Have a seat," she said, moving to offer me room next to her on the front porch swing. "Do you remember me? My name is Delores. How can I help you, Tallon?"

I told her everything I had experienced since my passing. She listened intently as I shared my experiences with her.

I had good intentions. I felt I had to do it to save Bryndle, but I feel so guilty for all the pain I have caused those still living in the physical world. I need help because I don't understand what is happening.

There was a long pause after my full disclosure, and I felt vulnerable in the silence. Finally, Delores spoke.

"I have to tell you, Tallon, that there is something special about you. I have never had such a clear conversation with a spirit before. What I think you are experiencing is a form of spirit warping. It works two different ways. For example, when someone you're deeply connected to is mourning your loss or they need you, you will feel them pulling at you. It also works the other way, when you're thinking of someone or feeling them and wanting to be with them. It's stronger right now because you have just passed over. As time goes by and your loved ones heal and find closure, the pull will diminish. After that happens, you can control the spirit warping by calling all your personal energy back to you and surrounding yourself in its white light to address their needs. You can connect with their energy, like you did with me today. As for the white light, you have already begun to figure out how to use it. Focus on what you want, and you will begin to better understand its power."

I am worried about Raya and all the pain I have caused her, I said, looking down guiltily at my feet. *Is she going to get her abilities back? Have I ruined her gift?*

"Tallon, we all have responsibility for our actions and reactions. I feel the two of you have a spiritual contract that you made before this life and that this is just the beginning of the work you promised to do together. You are both very special. We all have contracts. In fact, Tallon, you have contracts with many souls in this world...taking your life most likely cut some of those contracts short. Now, you will need to figure out how to fulfill those contracts from the spirit world."

You know what, to be honest, all I care about right now is saving my wife, I said, looking directly into her blue eyes.

She looked right back at me as if she was peering deep into my soul. I was spiritually exhausted, and she knew it. "Go, gather your energy, Tallon, and reflect on what we have talked about. I will take care of Raya. It may take some time, but we will figure it out. Until then, I do believe you have real friends in Winter and Ruby, and I sense that they will do anything to help you," she said as she gave me a hug. I was surprised I was able to feel her arms around me.

And with that, I relaxed as I understood the scope of the knowledge I needed to learn and master in this new realm. Recognizing that I needed some time alone to absorb what I had learned, I focused on the bench in the woods, and, like before, I found myself there. Shifting was getting easier. The bench was feeling more and more like home. It was my place for so many reasons. This forest had been here for me my whole life. The fragrant pine trees were like my family. The sound of the river and the falls was soothing. The area really resonated for me. I sat on the bench soaking up the moonlight and the forest's essence.

I understood that I was causing the warping of my soul to places here and there. I pulled all my energy back into me and focused on a real accounting of my thoughts and emotions. I needed to understand how my thoughts truly had power and direction. I spent most the night focusing my energy, and I wasn't pulled anywhere else.

I realized the way I had been approaching Bryndle was all wrong. I was trying to save her from what had happened—from an event that had taken place already and that I had no power to undo. What I needed to do was be with Bryndle, so she could allow me in and willingly give up her fight. I needed to stop creating more negative energy with my anger and shift my energy to more positive ends. If I could help calm or defuse the situation, perhaps Bryndle would see me and tell me her story. My hope was that in understanding the truth of her story, we could both see the present reality and find freedom together. My new plan was to allow Bryndle to direct me.

CHAPTER FIFTEEN

She Died Because of Me

I HAD MADE GREAT progress during the past few hours, and I could sense myself getting spiritually stronger. I had gained considerably more control of my energy and thoughts and thus where my spirit would go. I felt almost whole for the first time since I had died—like this was the real me. I no longer felt I could be uncontrollably pulled to a million different places. However, even with this spiritual growth, I still felt the painful void in me that was the loss of Bryndle and Oryan. Yet I now believed I was better equipped to help my family. I breathed in the heavenly smell of the pine trees and allowed my soul to call out to Bryndle.

I heard her running and breathing heavily and turned toward the sound. She was running next to the river, her murderer right behind her. He reached out and grabbed her long blond hair, pulling her down to pin her to the ground. As he began hitting her, she aggressively fought to defend herself and struggled back to her feet.

Even though I had consciously changed my mind on how I was going to approach the situation, I found my protective instincts kicking in once again, as I ran and tried to stop him. His fist went directly through me to strike her face. He continued to hit her about the face and head. I vainly tried to shield her as he continued to assault her. Her eyes were beginning to swell shut and blood dripped from her face. I watched in horror as she blacked out and fell to the ground only to regain consciousness and try to get back up. I had never seen that strength in another human being. She took blow after blow and continued fighting to live.

"Please, I will give you anything you want. You can have anything you want, just please don't hurt my baby," Bryndle gasped as she begged for mercy from her attacker.

My anger and my frustration grew. I repeatedly lunged between them to save her from pain. I couldn't help myself. It was my instinct to try to protect them. But, I couldn't, no matter how hard and desperately I tried.

He laughed at her pleas for her life. "You have nothing I want."

"Please don't, please, why are you doing this? Please don't hurt my baby," Bryndle cried.

"Beg me some more," he taunted. "I'm finding this all very amusing."

When he pulled out a knife, he laughed at the growing terror in Bryndle's face. That laugh sounded familiar, triggering a memory that refused to reveal itself. I couldn't place where I had heard that cold, triumphant laugh before.

Somehow, Bryndle, in her desperation to save her life and the life of our baby, managed to free herself again and run back into the forest. Each time she tripped on tree roots, she held tightly to her pregnant stomach, always trying to protect her baby.

"Mrs. Monroe, why are you making this so enjoyable for me? You think you can defy me, you little bitch? Go ahead. Keep running and fighting me. It just makes this more fun! Please, ask me to save your baby again," he said, bursting out again with that cold laugh.

"You know me? Who are you?" Bryndle asked fearfully as she tried to back away.

Oh, my God, Bryndle. He said our last name, he knows you, I said almost at the same time.

In her panic, Bryndle tripped on a rock and fell face-first into the snow. He smirked and lunged at her with his knife. Again, she quickly got back to her feet, but he grabbed her right leg to twist her body around and throw her back to the ground. She scratched his forearm as she fell.

"That was a mistake," he growled as he quickly struck at her protruding belly with the knife. She tried to block the descending blade with her arms and hands, and I watched as it sliced through her fingers, leaving two of them to dangle by a few shreds of skin. She managed to kick him in the face and rolled on her belly, trying once more to protect the baby. He seemed to ignore her weakening struggles as he relentlessly and repeatedly plunged the knife into her back. His intense anger escalated with an eerie calm that left him in complete control. Even when she knocked the knife out of his hands with her elbow and tried to get up again, he easily blocked her. Frantic, I tried to surround her with light and to call for help, but nothing worked.

That was when I realized I was doing it again. I was participating in the dark energy of what was happening to my wife. I knew I needed to be an observer and see what Bryndle wanted me to see. I needed to be stronger than I had ever been before. To have the courage not to interfere with what she was experiencing. To create a light within the darkness that she saw. I called my energy back and reminded myself through my tears that I needed to just be by Bryndle's side and allow her to take the lead. I felt strongly that she knew of my presence, even though there were no signs suggesting she was aware. In my heart, I was convinced she knew I was there. I proceeded with that conviction and paid attention to what she was showing me. I didn't want to miss an opportunity to help her or to hear her message.

Realizing that she could no longer get up and fearing that he would find the knife any minute, Bryndle tried to plead with him one more time. "Please, you don't have to do this. Please just spare my baby, she's due within a week. She can be saved even if I die, please stop for my baby's sake. I am begging you," she cried. Her voice was hoarse, and she was pale from loss of blood. She was nearing the end of her life.

Her attacker just laughed in pure enjoyment of her helplessness. "Why would I pass on a two for one?"

His response enraged Bryndle and she rallied to fight back, kicking him hard in the groin. "You will not hurt my baby! You have no right!"

Somehow, she made it back onto her feet even though she was trembling with growing weakness. I was humbled at how determined she was and so distraught at seeing her strength being tested to this degree. She finally sank to the ground, weakened from all the blood loss. He laughed hard and long at this, and my whole soul shook. I froze. Again, I knew that laugh. How did I know that laugh? My memories tried to surface, to show me his identity. I needed to see his face, but it was hidden by the black mask. I kept repositioning myself trying to get a better look, and then the moonlight caught his eyes, his glossed-over pale blue eyes.

Oh, my God, it's you, I cried out, as memories of him flooded into my mind.

I allowed those memories to pull me back into the past. I was at work again. I turned around to see myself trying to pull an angry young man away from the math teacher he had attacked. In seconds, everything went awry. He was so strong he took control as he pinned me, my past-self, to the ground. His soulless blue eyes glared at me the same way they were now glaring at Bryndle. They were glossy and emotionless. He laughed at me as I struggled to get up. He ripped my shirt open and I screamed for help as he attempted to pull off my pants. At the time, that was the most violence I had ever experienced. I elbowed him in the mouth, and as he bled, he laughed even harder. He continued to laugh as the staff finally restrained him.

Wesley Cavanaugh. Oh, my God, it was Wesley Cavanaugh. How could this have happened? But why, why did he go after my family? The incident happened years ago. He was dangerous, more dangerous than any of us had assumed and he was out there somewhere, free, still a threat to society. Is this what Bryndle wanted me to see?

I was desperate to share my new-found information. I knew if I could somehow tell Detective Cunningham, he would know what to do. I tried to focus on him, on the police station, but I had a difficult time focusing because I just wanted to go back and be with Bryndle. I couldn't get the images of what was happening to her out of my mind. I couldn't help but question whether part of the reason Bryndle was imprisoned by the murder was because it was unresolved. I had to try to see if telling the detective who the murderer was would free her. I took several deep breaths, recalled my energy and put Bryndle's awful attack out of my mind.

I tried to focus solely on Detective Cunningham but found myself in the forest once again. I understood why—my heart was here. This is where I wanted to be. I wanted to help Bryndle. But what if resolving her murder was the way to free her? I needed Detective Cunningham's help. I focused on him once again, armed with the knowledge Bryndle had shown me. The pine scent always helped to center me, so I took a deep breath to fill my lungs with the smell and refocused on Detective Cunningham.

Bryndle's scream broke my focus. How could I be expected to do this? How could I leave her side when she needed me the most? I, at least, needed to go to her and let her know that I had figured it out, and that I was trying to get help. She deserved nothing less. I envisioned Bryndle in the last place I had seen her and found myself right by her side. I knelt and gently placed my hand on her body, and I used my love to surround her in white light. I pictured the pure light entering and filling her every cell with my love for her. I pictured her safe and healthy. And then I spoke out loud to her, hoping she could hear me.

Bryndle, honey, I love you. You are safe. I know who is doing this to you, and I will take care of it. I'm right here, babe, and I am trying to help. I will tell Detective Cunningham everything.

I prayed she could hear me, even though she had shown no sign of being aware I was there. I prayed my love for her was starting to reach her. Now, to make good on my promise, I closed my eyes and connected with Detective Cunningham's energy. Instantly, I was taken to his home. He was sitting at the edge of his bed, sobbing into the arms of his wife. I had never seen him cry like this. I felt I was infringing on a delicate moment and turned to leave when I heard him speak.

"This is my fault. I should have done more. I must have missed something," he told his wife. "I failed her."

"Failed her? Honey, you have made this case your whole life. You work that case day and night. You've never given up, not even when everyone else in the department did. You are an excellent detective, and you approach your job with honor and integrity. You are a good man. She just missed her wife and baby and that's an indescribable loss, honey. Her suicide has nothing to do with you. This was about Tallon and her broken heart," his wife said, trying to console him as she held him in her arms.

No, it wasn't, I said as if they could hear me. *I know who the killer is Detective Cunningham. It's Wesley Cavanagh!*

I stood there looking at them and there was absolutely no sign either of them had any idea I was even in the room. His emotions weighed on me. I had caused so much pain to so many people. Suicide is difficult for people to understand. For some reason, they feel responsible. I felt guilty at how my actions had caused him so much self-doubt. I needed his help. I knew if I could just get through to Detective Cunningham, he would know what to do. But, how could I? What was I going to do? I sat on the edge of the bed, feeling helpless. I waited for him to fall asleep and repeatedly whispered everything I knew into his ear. I needed to believe he could hear me on some level. I needed someone to know who the murderer was, and I just didn't know how or who could understand me. The next morning, I waited around to see if I had made any progress with him.

"How did you sleep, sweetheart?" his wife asked as she put on her robe.

"Not very well, I had a restless night. My mind just wouldn't shut off," Detective Cunningham said.

"That's not surprising, honey. You are emotionally distraught right now, carrying a burden that isn't yours to bear. I'm sorry you didn't sleep well. I love you," she said, kissing his forehead before she walked out of the bedroom.

"I love you, too," he said quietly.

So, the only level of success I had was disturbing a good man's sleep. Detective Cunningham had no idea that I had been trying to communicate with him all night. How, oh, how was I going to get this information to the other side?

CHAPTER SIXTEEN

Light Versus Dark

TIME WAS TICKING AS I remained uncertain about my options. I knew Raya couldn't hear me and Delores had said it would take time before Raya's powers returned. As for Delores, I knew she was focusing on Raya, and I didn't want to disrupt that in any way if I didn't need to. I had caused so much pain. Then, I thought of Winter and Ruby, who Delores had confirmed had good intentions. Suddenly, I was hopeful. I needed to let someone know who the killer was, and maybe I could use their EVP, if I could just figure out how to make it work.

As I shifted to Winter and Ruby's home, I found them in bed sleeping. The love they shared was magnificent and I smiled as I watched them snuggle next to one another. It made me miss Bryndle even more and the way she used to hold me so close at night.

I walked down the stairs to the living room where Winter had left the EVP recorder. I found it running, just as they had promised. They really were true friends. I hesitated for a moment, and then I spoke into the recorder as clearly as I could.

The murderer is Wesley Cavanagh. He was a client at the adolescent treatment facility where I used to work. He was a resident there about five years ago. Again, the murderer's name is Wesley Cavanagh.

Converting my energy into words that could be heard on the digital voice recorder was difficult and new to me. I was exhausted, and I wasn't sure if it had worked. I waited for the recorder to alert them that I had left a message. After a few seconds, it beeped. I heard Winter and Ruby stirring upstairs. Oh, my gosh, it seemed to be working!

I heard Ruby calling out. "We're on our way down, Tallon. If that's you, please don't leave. We will be right there, honey. We need to know that you are okay."

I stood and waited as they entered the living room in their bath robes. "Oh, please Tallon, let this be you," Ruby said as she pressed the play button on the recorder.

It was hard to hear my voice through the static, and my message didn't come through at all as I had planned.

Murderer...white noise...*Wesley*...white noise... was all that came through.

Damn it, I suck at this! I screamed in frustration, disappointed that even with all my energy, my message hadn't come through completely.

"That's Tallon, Winter...I'm pretty sure that's Tallon! She's trying to communicate with us!"

"It must be important, but I'm not sure I'm understanding the whole message. Play it again, Ruby."

As they listened a second time, they looked at one another in confusion.

"Is she saying the murderer's name?" Winter asked Ruby.

"Yes, she is! Play it again," she responded.

"Wesley?" they asked one another.

"Tallon, is this Wesley guy the one who killed Bryndle?" Winter asked me, hoping I could hear him.

"Of course it is, Winter," Ruby said. "That's what she said."

"I know, Ruby, but what are we going to do with just a first name? Start a personal investigation of all the Wesleys in the world?" Winter asked in frustration. "I just want to help."

"I know, I know. The detective, that detective we met at the candlelight vigil, perhaps he can help. Maybe the name could be a lead?" Ruby suggested.

"That's a long-shot, honey. How are we even going to present it to him? Do we say we are talking with the dead and we need your help with a lead?" Winter asked, mockingly.

"I don't know, but we have to try," Ruby insisted.

"You're right, we need to at least try."

"Tallon, honey, we got your message," Ruby said into the room. "We are going to see if we can get this lead to the detective on the case. Even so, if you can give us anything else that would help, please do. I know it's hard to communicate, and it takes a lot of energy, but keep trying. We will do what we can but try to give us more information or some evidence. I'm not sure that this will be enough."

I knew they were right, that even with a full name, they needed evidence or some proof that Wesley was guilty. What if I could get him to confess? Could I do that? Could I get him to tell the truth? I leaned and spoke into the digital voice recorder a little slower, using fewer words and more concentrated energy. *Thank you. I will try.* I heard it replay as *thank...*white noise...*try.* Seriously, I didn't understand why this was so difficult.

Then, I concentrated on Wesley Cavanagh. I sensed the weight of his energy and shifted, finding myself in the courtroom following the incident at the facility. I recognized I was in the past again and was perplexed as to why I hadn't been pulled into the present. I decided I must be here for a valid reason, so I sat on a courtroom bench and watched as the proceedings unfolded once again.

Judge James, an honorable, intelligent woman, was asking my past self if I wanted to press charges. I remember the trepidation I felt that day. I had reviewed Wesley's files and was aware of the sexual abuse and neglect he had endured as a child. I felt sorry for him, even though he was at our facility for sexually assaulting two young girls. He looked like a choir boy that day in court, with his short blond hair and innocent eyes. I believed he needed a higher-level facility, not a lifetime of incarceration, a place where he might be cured, not just punished. So many studies have indicated prison often turns juvenile perpetrators into confirmed criminals, but that with proper treatment before they turn eighteen there is a possibility to change their behavior for the better. Our society let this child down by not taking him out of an abusive situation when he was younger, I told myself. He deserved a chance at rehabilitation.

"I do not believe pressing criminal charges now would be beneficial for Wesley," I told Judge James. "My recommendation is for him to be placed at a higher level of care such as a psychiatric residential treatment facility that specializes in these types of severe behaviors."

The judge accepted my recommendation and sent him to a facility in Idaho that offered treatment for violent behaviors and sexual deviance. He was only thirteen at the time of the court proceedings and would stay there until his eighteenth birthday. It was a similar facility to ours, but it dealt with more aggressive sexual behaviors. It was considered a lock-down facility and had a staff ratio of two to one. I believed this setting would allow him to have more structure and supervision and thus give him a better chance at rehabilitation.

I watched his reaction to the judge's decision. He was angry and glared at me with hatred. That was when I realized in horror that he would have just turned eighteen and been out of treatment for barely a few weeks when he murdered my wife and baby.

Time seemed to fast forward, as I saw Wesley admitted to the new treatment center in Idaho. His transition to this new setting was difficult, and I saw him beaten and harassed by the other patients, many of them older, much larger and stronger. I felt the pain he endured as the older boys on his unit picked on him daily and deliberately hit him where the bruises would not show. Incredibly, the staff overlooked these attacks, perhaps because of his history of attacking staff at my facility. They knew what had happened to me, and they hated him for it. Their callous attitude wouldn't have happened at my facility, but they obviously did not have the same clinical approach to treating troubled kids.

They forced the kids to behave by threatening severe consequences and sometimes the staff even beat the kids into compliance. This, coupled with the fact that the other boys could bully and attack him, just increased Wesley's anger and resentment. He blamed me for his being there and didn't understand that I had made that decision because I had his best interests at heart. He also refused to take responsibility for his own actions. I watched him write *I hate Tallon Monroe* repeatedly in a notebook. As the years passed and the abuse he suffered increased, so did his hatred toward me.

By the time he was sixteen, Wesley started talking to his roommate about killing me. He became obsessed with this thought and planned everything down to the last detail. It was around this time that I witnessed five young men in his unit sexually assault him. One staff member was present and pretended not to see. What happened to him was awful, unspeakable. I felt so bad for my role in sending him to such a horrible program.

After this attack, Wesley obsessively began working out to make himself stronger and better able to protect himself. The trauma the young man suffered made him callous and dangerous. He had been well taught that adults were not to be trusted and that no one cared about his welfare. By the time he was eighteen, he was muscular and large in stature, completely unstable emotionally, and even more violent than he had been before. He walked out of the facility on his eighteenth birthday with only one thought in mind—seeking revenge for what he believed I had done to him.

During the years, everything had become my fault in his mind. Even simple things, like breaking a pencil during class, became my fault. If he did poorly on a test, it was my fault. If he didn't get dinner because he had been involved in a fight—a punishment clearly violating patient rights—it was my fault. He was obsessed with blaming me and not once did he ever take responsibility for his own actions. His justification for the acts he committed deeply troubled me. All he had endured did not give him the right to murder my wife and child.

Before Bryndle's murder, I had been convinced that all people were good at heart, but the awful reality is that some people are broken and cannot be redirected from traveling a dark path. Terrible guilt and regret rested heavily on my soul. I wondered if I could have changed the course of his life by holding him responsible for his actions when he attacked me. Perhaps the best thing would have been to press charges, but when you are dealing with children, it's just so difficult to know the right thing to do. You question everything. You ask, do they just need structure and to know that someone cares? Or, are they beyond repair with no hope of rehabilitation? I had tried to give him a chance, but what I really did was take away any hope for a normal future.

As I thought about him and everything that had happened to him, I shifted again. This time the warping took me to an unfamiliar house. I looked around and spotted Wesley on the couch watching television and drinking a beer. An elderly lady sat at the kitchen table all alone in the dark. This must be the present, I thought. I walked closer to the couch and just watched him for a moment. He must be about twenty-one-years old now, I thought. Knowing he had already committed that horrible crime against my family filled me with an intense anger and a disdain that I had never felt before for another human being.

To keep my feelings from taking over, I looked around at the environment he lived in. It was obvious from the dated pictures on the wall and the faded, flowered pattern of the living room wallpaper that he was living with his grandmother, the only family member I could recall that was ever involved in his life, and her presence had been sporadic at best. She was small and frail and, judging from the pile of medicine bottles on the kitchen counter, was obviously sick.

Wesley startled me as he came into the kitchen to get another beer. "What are you doing in here, old lady? Go to your room. It creeps me out when you just sit there and look off to space like that, you crazy bitch." When she didn't move or acknowledge what he was saying, he slapped her across the face. I jumped back in shock. "Did you hear me, old lady? I said go to your room," he snarled at her.

She held her hand to her cheek and as he raised his arm to strike her again, she cowered. "Please don't hit me, Wes, please," she said in a fearful and defeated tone.

"I'll hit you if I want," he yelled. "You don't get to tell me what to do. You deserve every beating I give you for telling on me when I was twelve and sending me to that damn treatment center. You know that girl wanted it."

He grabbed her arm and yanked her out of the chair. "Now go to your room!" he said, shoving her toward the hallway. She lost her balance, falling to the kitchen floor. Wesley just laughed as she painfully reached for the kitchen counter, grasping it for support as she struggled to stand.

How could someone be so cruel? There was a darkness around Wesley, an emptiness in his eyes that left me with the distinct impression that he did not have a soul. Unsure of what to do next or how to proceed, I just stood in the corner of the room and watched him, trying to gain an understanding of who he was now. He returned to the living room to watch television most of the evening.

The growing darkness of the moonless night seemed to energize Wesley—although the forces sparking in him made me shiver. His eyes were alert. The normally slouched-over young man stood tall with confidence and determination. He seemed aroused about something as I followed him to his bedroom, curious to know the focus of his energy. His bedroom was surprisingly organized and well-kept, unlike the rest of the house. He quietly shut his door behind him and walked to his window to pull his curtains closed.

He looked around the room, as if to make one last check that no one would see him and got down on his hands and knees to pull a box from under his bed. It appeared to be a large hat box, probably belonging to his grandmother. It was round with a floral print on the top. It looked old and worn. He caressed the top of the box and gently brushed away any dust that had gathered on it, as if it were his most prized possession and he wanted it to be perfect before he opened it.

I watched him carefully take out several articles of clothing. He lifted each item to his face and inhaled their scent with long deep breaths. His eyes glossed and glittered with stimulation. I witnessed Wesley methodically unfold the clothes and gently lay them out on his bed. Everything he did, the enjoyment on his face, the ceremonious manner as he approached the items in the box, all made me uneasy. And then a horrifying realization dawned—these were the clothes he had worn the night he killed Bryndle and Oryan.

He kept the clothes. *Why would he do that? Why would he take such a risk?* I thought as I stood there dumbfounded. Then I answered my own questions—he had kept the clothing because they were mementos that had great meaning for him. Consequently, keeping them was worth the risk. It had been more than three years since the murders, and I could tell by the smirk on his face that he believed he had gotten away with it.

At least now I knew evidence existed that could link him to the murders. I was shaken to my core by the discovery. How did I not see the depth of evil that existed in him? I needed to let Detective Cunningham know as soon as possible what Wesley had just unsuspectingly revealed.

As I focused my thoughts on Detective Cunningham, a sudden increase in local energy pulled me back to Wesley. His energy had deepened into darkness, a darkness that I somehow recognized as the same blackness that surrounded Wesley when he murdered Bryndle and Oryan. As this darkness intensified, I could sense his growing anticipation and excitement.

What is happening? I turned to look at Wesley. He slowly undressed and then put on the same clothing he wore when he murdered my wife and baby. He quietly left the house, decked out in the dark black coat, dark T-shirt, and jeans, carrying the ski mask. I knew this couldn't be good. I couldn't leave now. I had to see what he was up to. As I trailed him, his energy expanded and his aura turned a revolting, roiling gray streaked with flashes of red. I could tell he intended to hurt and perhaps kill someone. I wondered if his energy had always felt this dark in the lateness of night or was it enhanced and made even more evil by his ceremonious unveiling and wearing of the clothes.

A few blocks away from his house, he cut through an alley and crossed several lawns on the next street. He moved deliberately, and I knew he had made this trip before. He was looking for something or someone specific, and I found myself feeling uneasy. He approached an older home and stood quietly behind a tree near the edge of the property. He looked at his watch and counted out loud, "Three, two, one," and the sprinklers that had been running turned off. He walked silently, confidently, toward the house and seemed to disappear into the landscaping along the side of the house. Reaching the back, he turned toward the rear porch.

I couldn't help but wonder if this was how Wesley had hunted Bryndle. Who or what was he hunting now? A potted plant sat near the back door. He bent down, quietly tilted it and retrieved a key from underneath. I moved closer. I needed to know what was going on. After grabbing the key, he sat the pot back in its proper place. He slowly straightened and then walked off the porch to return to the tree on the front lawn and to continue watching the house. He looked down at his watch again. "And now," he said as the sprinklers closest to the back deck came on. Wesley patiently waited for the sprinklers to finish their cycle, and then walked to the other side of the house. I followed.

Halfway around, there was a set of stairs leading to the basement door. Wesley quietly stepped down the stairs and used the key to open the door. He moved like a ghost, silently slipping inside and up the basement stairs to the interior of the house. He passed the bedrooms and walked to the front door to unlock the deadbolt and door. He turned and headed back toward the bedrooms. He appeared to be in his element. He stopped outside the bedroom on the right side of the hallway. Its door was closed, and a placard bore the words, Riley's Room, written in pink.

Oh, my God! I thought. *What is he doing?* I couldn't let anything happen to Riley. I slipped through the wall into the bedroom. I saw a little girl in her pajamas snuggled up in bed with her dolls. She appeared to be about five years old. I could hear Wesley slowly opening her door. Each time the door creaked he would pause, and then continue to push it open inch by inch. I panicked. I had to get this baby to safety. Hysterical, I tried to push the door shut, but I just fell through both the door and Wesley. I refocused my energy and, jumping back into the bedroom, I tried to enter Riley's mind through her dreams, shouting to her to wake up. Somehow, it worked as she sat up in her bed and looked directly at me. It was evident that she saw me, but I wasn't sure she could hear me.

Riley, is that your name?

She nodded.

Riley, honey, everything is going to be okay, I am here to help you, and I need you to listen very closely, I said as I tried to keep my panic to a minimum.

"Are you an angel?" she asked.

Riley, I need you to scream for your parents louder than you have ever screamed before. Can you do that for me?

She shook her head, beginning to become frightened.

Riley, please. There is a very bad man trying to get in your room, and I need you to scream and wake up your parents. I'm trying to keep you safe, honey. Please do it for me.

She looked at the door and saw it slowly inch open. Her eyes widened at the realization of what was happening. Riley's scream broke through the silence of the night.

"Daddy! Help! Help! There's a man coming in my room!"

Riley's bedroom door slammed shut and I could hear Wesley running to the front of the house. He obviously had prepared his exit plan and fled out the front door. Within seconds, another set of feet ran toward the front door, and I heard a man yell, "Stop! Maggie, call the police!" as he ran out of the house in pursuit.

Riley's mother ran into her daughter's bedroom. She scooped Riley up and took her with her as she retrieved her cell phone and called the police.

"Mommy an angel was in my room."

"That wasn't an angel, sweetheart, that was a bad man," the mother said, still in a panic.

"No, the angel saved me from the bad man," Riley insisted.

Knowing that Riley was safe, I now needed to find Wesley. I followed his energy to the alley where Riley's dad had caught and tackled him. They were wrestling fiercely on the ground. Riley's dad tore Wesley's ski mask off during the altercation, but the dark hid his facial features. As the father tossed the mask to the side, Wesley forcefully punched him, and Riley's dad fell back, unconscious. It was the same sort of punch that I saw Wesley deliver multiple times to Bryndle. Wesley sprang to his feet and frantically looked around for his mask. I heard a neighbor come outside, awakened by the noise. Wesley heard him too, and, forced to abandon his search, took off running. As soon as I knew the neighbor was rushing to help Riley's dad, I followed Wesley back to his house.

Wesley ran inside, locked the door and quickly turned off the lights. He paced back and forth, clearly panicked. Not so much in his element anymore, I thought to myself.

"No, no, I can't believe this. I've got to think, and I've got to think fast," Wesley spoke out loud and then walked into his grandmother's room to wake her up.

"Grandma, did you take your meds?" He turned on her light and spoke in a completely calm voice, showing none of his earlier distress. "I'm sorry, Grandma. I fell asleep and forgot to give them to you. I'm just so tired after all the work I did mowing the lawn and all for you."

"Yes, Wes, you already gave them to me, my sweet boy," his grandmother said sleepily, happy to receive caring attention from him. She did not realize it was feigned nor did she notice the clothes he wore.

"Oh, okay, I just needed to make sure you were okay. Go back to sleep, Grams," he said, turning out her light and shutting her door as he left the room.

Back in his own bedroom, he removed his hunting clothes, folded them neatly, put them back in his special box, and returned it to its hiding place under his bed. Then he took a shower.

That was too close, I said to myself, still trembling. *How dare he?* Wesley Cavanagh is a dangerous man and needs to be stopped. My mind swirled with so many emotions. I saw flashes of what he had done to Bryndle and our baby. I couldn't stop thinking about Riley and what he had almost accomplished earlier this night. I knew he was dangerous. After his shower, he sat on the couch and turned on the television, as if nothing had happened. After a few minutes, he fell into a deep sleep.

How could he sleep? This is so unfair! Riley's family just had their whole life turned upside down. Their house had been invaded and Riley's dad was probably in the hospital. That little girl had almost been taken or worse. How would Riley ever understand tonight's events? Her innocence had just been ripped away. How could she ever feel safe in her bed again? And my family—he took everything from me and held a ceremony tonight to revel in the details and to commit yet another crime. My emotions continued to roil at thoughts of Bryndle and everything my sweet wife had endured.

With these thoughts, I unintentionally shifted away from Wesley and was pulled back to the forest. The murder had already occurred, and her smoldering body lay under the pine tree. I was still failing her. I knelt next to her burned, tortured, and nearly unrecognizable body and held her in my arms. I mourned for her as I whispered, *I'm here. I'm right here with you, love.* I surrounded her body in my loving light, but I couldn't find or sense her spirit anywhere. Did she even know I was there? Would I ever be able to free her from this nightmare? While she was enduring all of this, Wesley was sleeping without a conscience, without any remorse. In fact, this heart-breaking image of Bryndle's completed murder was probably the image that gave him comfort.

My fury and frustration exploded, and I found myself standing right next to him in his living room. He was still deep asleep on the couch. I stood there wondering, what to do with him, about the whole situation. To my surprise, I found myself inside his mind, listening to his thoughts and dreams. To my horror, I watched as he basked in the memories and details of killing Bryndle. Each time he did a play-by-play of how he took her life, I felt the satisfaction, the adrenalin rush it gave him. Being able to see and feel his every pleasure made me loathe him even more.

Something in my soul warned me to leave his mind, that it was dangerous to be caught in the evil of this dark energy. However, just as I decided to leave, he began dreaming about his desire to do his evil yet again to the little girl, to Riley. I saw all the horrific things he intended for her. I felt his uncontrollable need and hunger to prey on the vulnerable and I was suffocated by his evil. I could not stay in his mind for one more minute. I could feel a thick darkness creeping closer, all around me. Witnessing such malevolent actions and thoughts made me feel dirty and somehow an accomplice. I panicked and struggled to get out of his mind. I focused on the living room and manifested in front of his physical body. I vomited his dark energy across the front room as my soul tried to cleanse and purge itself of his evil.

Sickened and overwhelmed emotionally at the intensity of his malicious inner thoughts and desires, I collapsed into an armchair. I did not yet understand these abilities, my new mind-jumping power, nor was I ready for the impact the core of his darkness might have on my soul. I shook violently. It was so unnatural to experience this evil. How could humanity have gotten this lost? I now knew, without a doubt, that this man's soul was pure evil. I lost myself in an enraged fury—all I could think about was that I wanted him to feel everything he had put my wife through. I wanted him to feel the fear, the torturous pain, the desperation and panic before he died himself.

You're not resting until my wife rests! I yelled as I kicked at the couch. I did it with so much fury and force, the couch actually moved. Wesley stirred, and I tapped into a new and unfamiliar source of energy. I felt justified and powerful. The need for vengeance consumed me.

As I stood there looking at this man and thinking about what he had taken from me, what he could have taken from Riley's family that night, what he might take from some other family tomorrow, I reveled in my growing anger. I paid no heed to another warning from my soul. I lunged at him and began choking him. He awoke gasping for breath, as his arms tried to pull away the unseen force that was clamped around his throat. His eyes were wide open and full of fear. He couldn't see me, but I had no doubt he could physically feel my presence, my fury, my desire to hurt him.

I released him after only a few seconds and stepped back in awe at what I had just done. Violence wasn't part of my being. It was a new experience for me, but in that moment, in that rage, I didn't really care. I stood there, shocked at my ability to physically interact with the living world. I looked down at my hands trying to make sense of it all.

He coughed for a few minutes, holding his neck and looking around, confused and trying to make sense of what had happened. I could tell I had terrified him. Turning the tables on him felt good. I smiled as he jumped at every noise within the house. He reeked of fear. I admit, part of me enjoyed it, and I wanted him to feel even more afraid. But deep inside I was terrified by my own emotions and my enjoyment of the situation. Nevertheless, caught up in the moment, all I knew was that finally, I could make him pay.

As I watched him, I realized I could kill him, and this realization frightened me. What was I becoming? Even so, I knew I could not stop. I focused on the beer can, sitting on the coffee table next to him, and it flew across the room. Wesley jumped up in a panic. I yanked a picture off the wall behind him and it crashed to the floor. He turned around, and I threw another picture in his direction. He ducked out of its way in sheer horror.

This was my rampage. This was my vengeance. I jumped to the kitchen and opened the cupboard, running my arm under the stacked dishes. They crashed to the floor. I opened and closed drawers and threw silverware at Wesley. He hid behind the couch and cried as he huddled on the floor in a fetal position. I flickered the lights on and off and rattled the chandelier. Wesley cowered, covering his face with his hands and arms.

Images of Bryndle's charred body filled my mind—my beloved wife and baby tortured and taken from me before their time. I crept behind Wesley and shoved his head into the back of the couch. His face hit the edge of the couch leg with such force that it split his upper lip. Blood dripped from his mouth, but it was nothing compared to all blood that had covered Bryndle's face. In shock, he jumped up to his feet and held his bleeding mouth. My fist flew with a massive uppercut to his chin. He slammed backward against the wall from the force of my punch.

"Stop! Who's there, who's doing this? Coward, show yourself!"

How dare you yell at me? I shouted at Wesley. I shoved him hard and grabbed his hair while I hit him again with a left jab that broke the skin above his eye. Blood poured down his face and even that sight didn't make me pause.

Scared, he frantically looked around in every direction, spinning his body about as if he could ward off the invisible attacker. A thought spoke in my mind asking if this was fair, that he couldn't even see his attacker. Was it fair the way he dominated Bryndle and taunted her so?

Was it fair what he did to her, how he tortured her? Was it fair that he ended a life before it was even born? I countered.

I kicked him hard between the legs. He fell to the ground clutching his groin in anguish, gasping for breath. Empowered, I circled around him as if I was deciding how to finish him off. Trembling and in pain, he slowly stood up. I saw that he had soiled his pants and it exhilarated me. Consumed with my relentless slaughter, I delivered a savage kick to his head. He flew across the room and hit the living room window. The window shattered as he fell to the floor amidst the broken glass. Then I heard a noise behind me. It was his grandmother crying out in fear.

"What is happening? Wesley, are you okay?" she called from the hallway. I could tell she couldn't make sense of what she saw. When he didn't move, I watched her cautiously move to his side. "Wesley?" He didn't answer, and I watched as she clutched him and rocked him back and forth in her arms. I had completely forgotten that she was in the house.

I slowly approached and saw that Wesley was still breathing, that he was just unconscious. I watched as his grandmother held him, crying, calling for him to come back, telling him she was right there with him— just the way I had held Bryndle only a few minutes ago. Afraid and looking around at the house's disarray, she cried even louder. She was so confused. Seeing her pain and utter fear of the unknown made me ashamed. What had I done? What was I doing?

I felt my knees weaken and I sank to the floor in a corner of the room. I looked at the blood on my hands. I thought of Bryndle. What would she think of my actions? I thought of what she had endured and about everything we once shared. I kept thinking of all the different memories we had made together—the Saturday mornings we went hiking and how she so enjoyed nature she would stop every few feet to take a picture. It was annoying, but so beautiful to see her engaged in the moment. She spent so much time taking pictures, we rarely had time to finish our hikes.

I thought of the mornings we would wake up early, before the rest of the world, to brew a fresh batch of coffee. We would go out on the deck and snuggle up under a blanket to sip our warm coffee and watch the sunrise. Those moments felt so perfect. I chuckled to myself when I thought about how she would surprise me with breakfast in bed on my birthday—the omelet she made was frankly disgusting, but I tried so hard to eat it. All these memories made me smile, and I felt love enter my soul like it never had before. There she was. Bryndle's love was pulling me back.

I realized that somehow, I had unintentionally channeled Wesley's dark energy. Tapping into his mind had not left me unscathed. What I had just done was wrong. It wasn't true to me. It wasn't who I chose to be or how I wanted to grow spiritually. I knew in a practical sense that it was natural to be angry with Wesley, but vengeance and retaliation were not mine to seek. I wanted justice and needed to better understand what I had just allowed to happen. I needed to center myself, to connect with my higher self, so I retreated to my bench in the woods.

Nature never fails in quieting my soul. It allowed me to seek answers inside myself about why I had just harmed another human being. I realized that attaching so emotionally to Wesley's mind had left me susceptible to his dark energy with no ability to guard myself against its power. I had allowed Wesley's energy to enter my being. My soul had tried to purge itself of that dark force, knowing that light and dark cannot exist together. Nevertheless, my emotions had clung to its power and it fed my anger, my fear, my rage. I allowed that darkness to take control of me, and I could never let that happen again. I was careless in permitting this negative energy into my soul and in allowing it to influence my actions. Having the ability to call on such powerful energy was a huge responsibility. I needed to be true to myself. The energy I had allowed to overcome my soul was the same energy Wesley used when he committed his horrible acts. I wanted no association with it.

I'm sorry. I'm so sorry for what I have done, I sobbed. This realization had a surprising spiritual impact on me. By acknowledging my mistake and expressing my willingness to take accountability, I found I could absorb even more light and love into my soul.

I humbly made a mental note of everything I had learned. I did not understand my abilities yet and resolved to be cautious. I realized the importance of always protecting my energy field, of the need to be vigilant about the light. This knowledge increased my awareness that even in death, I could make serious mistakes. Death was providing me a series of opportunities to learn. I could either grow or stagnate. I could choose which energy source to align with—the choice had always been mine.

I went back to Wesley's house to check on him. He had come back to consciousness and I knew that he was going to be all right. Nevertheless, the terror I had caused his grandmother was irreversible. I knew that what I was capable of would not help Bryndle. To free Bryndle and save other potential victims, it was my responsibility to bring Wesley to justice in the right way.

Ann and Michele Modtland

CHAPTER SEVENTEEN

Earthly Justice

DETECTIVE CUNNINGHAM KEPT ENTERING my thoughts. I felt he, more than anyone, could help me in bringing Wesley to justice the right way. I decided to visit him, desperate for his help.

I watched Detective Cunningham sleep. He was twitching, sweating and in the thrall of a bad dream. I could sense him thinking about me and Bryndle and Oryan. His sadness was as deep as ever, and it was almost as if he were aware of my presence on some level. He stirred and turned on his back.

"Can't sleep again, sweetheart?" his wife whispered.

"I'm sorry," he said, opening his eyes. "Am I keeping you awake? I just have so much on my mind. Something really strange happened today, and I can't get it off my mind."

"What happened, babe?" she asked.

"I met two of Tallon's friends months ago at a candlelight vigil. Tallon seemed to think highly of them. You remember Winter and Ruby?"

"Yes, I do. They were a nice couple."

"That's what I thought too...well, they stopped by to see me today at the station. They told me that they had been in communication with Tallon from the other side, and that she wants me to check on a man named Wesley. Can you believe that? And it's just a first name. How is that supposed to lead me to anyone? The thing is, they are probably delusional, right?"

His wife was quiet for a moment. "But you can't shake the feeling that there might be something to it?"

"Yeah, I can't help but wonder. I can't really go knocking on every man's door who's named Wesley, but maybe I can bring up the name to the family and see if it means anything."

"I don't think you will forgive yourself if you don't. It might not be anything, but you need to be sure."

"You're right. Thanks, honey, I will stop by and talk to them tomorrow."

I couldn't believe it, Winter and Ruby did it! I was positive my mother and father would remember who Wesley was. We had talked about that case in detail. My dad was deeply concerned about the behaviors Wesley displayed during his attack on me. He had counseled me and given me his professional opinion about Wesley's actions.

With a sense of hope, and a knowledge that I couldn't really do much more this late at night, I left to check on Riley and her family. They were at the hospital as the sun rose. Riley's dad, Tom, had suffered a concussion and a few broken ribs, but he was going to be fine and the hospital was getting ready to release him. I watched Riley asleep on her mother's lap as the mother stroked her hair. Such beauty in the innocence of a child, I thought to myself. Thank God, she was safe.

Then I heard Tom talking to the discharge nurse. "Yes. I filed a police report and gave my statement as well. I'm just so angry he got away from me. I couldn't give a good description of his face, though, because it was so dark. When I had him on the ground and we were fighting, I was able to tear off his ski mask and the police did recover it. I'm a pretty big guy but he got away from me. The police mentioned they would check the face mask for a strand of hair or something with DNA on it. The officer said its highly likely they will find his DNA, especially since it was a face mask and it would be saturated with his sweat and saliva. I'm just so thankful he didn't get my little girl and that the police are taking this seriously. If they have a record of his doing this before, they will be able to get him. I can't believe he was after my baby girl. I just hope and pray they get him," he said as he looked down at Riley. "In the meantime, my daughter won't leave my sight."

Oh, my gosh, they recovered the ski mask! I bet there would be blood on that mask that will link him to Bryndle and Oryan's murder, too. This could be the evidence I was looking for, the break we needed to put Wesley away for good. *I must tell Detective Cunningham.*

By the time I returned to the detective, he was in his office working on his computer. I saw by the paperwork spread across his desk that he was preparing a proposal for a court order to release all admission records from my work for all patients with the first name of Wesley. He must have met with my parents that morning, and they must have pointed him in the right direction. Of course, they wouldn't have known Wesley's last name, since I don't think I ever mentioned it to them. Getting the court to release these types of records—especially treatment records from our facility—is near impossible, especially without a reasonable cause implicating Wesley in the murders. The medical records team would deny the request, citing federal HIPAA privacy laws.

I knew Detective Cunningham was trying to investigate based on limited information. We did not have the time for all these formalities, so I needed to help him out. I tried to commandeer his keyboard and type out his last name but couldn't get the keyboard to respond. I can do this. I can figure this out, I told myself. I closed my eyes and as I envisioned gathering more positive energy, the lights in the office flickered. As Detective Cunningham looked around, a little puzzled, I tapped into a larger source of energy—perhaps enough to be more successful. I focused my new energy and again tried to type. The sound of keys clicking on the keyboard captured Detective Cunningham's attention. He lifted his arms off the desk, to stare in surprise at his keyboard.

It's working, I thought to myself, as the letters I was typing appeared on the monitor's screen.

This is Tallon Monroe. Wesley Cavanagh killed Bryndle and Oryan.

He jumped up, his eyes darting around the room. "Tallon, is that really you?" His breathing was rapid and shallow. "You really are trying to communicate with the living, aren't you?" he whispered, lowering his voice to ensure no one else could hear him.

I wanted to exchange pleasantries and give him time to absorb the fact that I really was communicating with him from the other side before I told him the rest. But the truth was, I didn't have the time or the energy to do that, so I continued typing.

Yes, it's me. Wesley Cavanagh murdered Bryndle and Oryan. He tried to attack a child last night. Police report made. Ski mask found— should connect him to murders.

"Okay, Tallon, I'm not going to lie. I am freaking out right now, but for some reason, I believe it's you and not some sick joke. Call it intuition or gut instinct, but, umm, I got your message from Winter and Ruby, and your parents told me there was a Wesley in treatment where you worked, and that he attacked you."

Detective Cunningham slowly sat back down in his chair and continued to talk to the computer screen. "He, this Wesley, tried to attack a child last night? I have been in my office all morning researching the name Wesley and I haven't been briefed on last night's events yet. Is there any further information you can give me?"

5th East and Maple, I typed.

"Okay, let me see what I can find. I'll pull that case and look it over."

He stood up and even though he couldn't see me, he offered me his seat. *Such a kind- hearted man, even to the dead,* I joked to myself.

He leaned out of his office doorway and motioned for two detectives to join him.

"How can we help you, boss?" asked one.

"Bradley, what can you tell me about the report of an attempted kidnapping on Maple Street last night?" Detective Cunningham asked.

Bradley was a young female officer with a baby face. She reminded me of Emi but was tall, with dark hair and dark eyes. "I was called out to the scene last night and just finished writing up my report," she said. "A man broke into the house and attempted to enter a five-year-old's room around one thirty last night. The parents woke when their daughter screamed for help. The dad chased the intruder out of the home, while the mom secured the daughter and called 911.

"Dad and the intruder ended up in an altercation in the alley adjacent to the house, and before the dad was knocked unconscious, he was able to pull a ski mask off the intruder. A neighbor heard the commotion and came out to see what was going on. He startled the perp, who ran off. Police were dispatched but were unable to apprehend him. The neighborhood was monitored for the remainder of the night with no solid leads. We were, however, able to retrieve the ski mask from the alley. It's in evidence right now. The dad was taken to the hospital for medical care, and after he was discharged early this morning, he and his wife came directly to the station to find out if there have been any new developments or leads. They are understandably concerned for the safety of their daughter."

"And this was on Maple Street, correct?"

"Yes," both officers answered.

Detective Cunningham paced back and forth, visibly distressed.

"Is everything OK, sir?" Detective Bradley asked.

"No, not really. I have a hunch. Detective Jones, will you make sure that ski mask is thoroughly checked for bloodstains old and new, fibers, hair, anything that can give us a lead."

"Yes sir, of course."

"Did the father say he could ID the perp? Did he or the daughter get a good look at him?"

"Not of his face, it was really dark in the alley. He did report that the man seemed young, was muscular, and had light hair, possibly blond," Jones responded.

Detective Cunningham walked to his desk and retrieved a piece of paper.

"Can you bring in Wesley Cavanagh for me? I would like to question him about his whereabouts last night. His address is seven six nine three West Willow Road.

"And, Jones, don't underestimate this man. I have reason to believe he is violent with women," he said, looking right at Bradley to make the point. Jones was in his mid-twenties and was a physically fit, military-looking man. "I will have Stacy prepare an interrogation room. I want Wesley Cavanagh to sit in there for a while."

"Understood, boss," Bradley said, and they left.

"Tallon, you still here?" Detective Cunningham asked.

Yes, I typed.

"Did you say something, boss?" Jones peeked back in.

"Nope." Embarrassed, he shut his door.

"You are going to get me in trouble, Tallon. People are going to think I have gone crazy. I mean I can't even believe you are here, myself." He let out a deep sigh. "Is there anything else you can think of, Tallon? Any information on the break-in that may be useful, like did he leave any other evidence behind?"

He keeps everything under his bed. Wesley used the same clothes he wore when he murdered Bryndle and Oryan, I typed. I was feeling weak but did my best to keep going. *I roughed him up a bit last night. Got a little out of control. I'm just so angry. It won't happen again. I don't want to be that person.*

"Hmm, don't be too hard on yourself. Honestly, I think he deserved it. I would like to punch him, myself."

I smirked. Detective Cunningham always made me feel better about myself, and I appreciated his calm and candid demeanor so much.

A young woman peered through his office window as she walked by and gave him a funny look. "Seriously, I look like I am going crazy, talking to you." He picked up his cell phone and pretended to talk into it.

What's your plan? I typed.

"I'll start with general questioning and see if he gives in under pressure. And in the interim, we will see what evidence we can pull from the ski mask. I wonder if I can get the judge who presided over the incident at your facility to release his records. If we can show a pattern of his behavior it might just help in the investigation."

Judge James was the presiding judge, I typed.

"Okay," he said, picking up his office phone. "Stacey, can you get the number for Judge James—Falls County I believe. That would be great, thank you."

As he was talking on the phone, I looked around his office. His desk was full of files and papers. To my surprise, I noticed that next to his computer monitor, along with a framed photo of his family, he had a photo of my family. It was a copy of the same picture that hung in our living room. Bryndle was eight months pregnant, radiant as ever, and sat alongside Chewy and me.

I looked at Detective Cunningham in awe. Shortly after he was assigned to the case, he asked for a family photo, vowing that it would stay on his desk until their murderer was brought to justice. I nodded my head slowly, realizing that he was a man of his word, full of integrity and kindness, that he used our picture as a reminder of the justice he intended to bring to the individual that had taken their beautiful lives in such a horrific way. I let out a deep breath and looked back at the detective. He seemed older today. His normally perfect hair was a little longer, and gray strands showed through. He had a little stubble on his chin and looked like he hadn't slept in days. A few minutes after his phone call with Stacey ended, the phone rang again.

"Hello, oh wow, that was fast. That's great, Stacey, thank you. Yes, please connect me.

"Yes, I am here. Hello, Judge James. Thank you so much for talking with me. My name is Detective Cunningham at the Pine Ridge Police Department. I am in the middle of a murder investigation, and I was hoping you could help me. I understand you were the presiding judge in a case about eight years ago that is of particular interest to me..."

"Hold on, please. I tried to go through archives, but this case involved a juvenile, and I believe the records are sealed."

I could only hear his side of the conversation, but I knew the judge was at least listening to him.

"The case was Tallon Monroe versus Wesley Cavanagh and involved an incident that took place at a residential treatment center about eight years ago. The young man, Wesley Cavanagh, would have been thirteen at the time..."

"Yes, your Honor, I understand he was a minor and his records are sealed. That's why I am calling..."

"Well, I have received an anonymous tip pertaining to a murder case I am working on, suggesting his possible involvement..."

"No, I have no physical evidence." He shook his head and his shoulders slumped.

"Wait. Judge James, please, the victim in that case, Mrs. Tallon Monroe, it's her wife and unborn child that were murdered. I have been on this case for three years now and received some viable information. A reliable source suggested the involvement of Wesley Cavanaugh. You are my only hope for getting his juvenile records as Mrs. Tallon Monroe is no longer alive, either..."

"Please, don't hang up, please hear me out. The Monroe murders took place about three years ago, near the frozen falls..."

"Oh, I didn't know you were aware of this case...Yes, your Honor, it was a heinous crime. That's why I need your help..."

"No, I didn't know you were friends with Tallon..."

"Yes, I know what that means. I'm sorry. I didn't realize you had worked together for so long. Yes, your Honor, I'm sorry for your loss. I have reason to believe that Wesley Cavanagh may have been involved in the Monroe murders. Wesley would have just turned eighteen a few months prior to the murders..."

"No, just the anonymous tip, your Honor, but if I can get his case file, I may be able to piece some things together and show a continuing pattern from his adolescent life that has continued into his adult life...to determine if it fits the profile..."

"Yes, I understand that there are certain criteria that need to be met..."

"Judge James, please, my gut tells me he is involved. Can't you do it for Tallon?

"Hello...Judge James..."

"No, wait. Please, can I at least meet with you and discuss some facts? Hello..."

"Damn it", he said, slamming the phone down.

He looked defeated. I grabbed the keyboard again.

It's okay, we have other things we can try, I typed.

"I know, Tallon, but those records really would have helped me build a case. I just don't understand the system sometimes."

I typed again. *He is abusive to his grandmother, maybe that angle can help? I have to go. Just think about me and call my name if you need me, I will feel you and come.*

I wanted to say I would work on Judge James, but I didn't want to give him false hope. I didn't know if I could reach her, but I decided to try. After all, I knew that whatever information was in Wesley's juvenile files would only help Detective Cunningham and give him a better understanding of who Wesley was and how his circumstances influenced his behavior. His juvenile crimes would show a pattern. All this information would help in the interrogation process as well.

Judge James was in her chambers alone when I arrived. It was a nice office, clean and orderly like herself. She was working on her computer, completely engrossed in her work. I had developed so much respect for Judge James when I had worked with her. She was a kind woman who took her job seriously and did it with integrity. When my wife and unborn baby were murdered, she took me to lunch and offered to help in any way she could. I knew it was hard to say no to Detective Cunningham, but she was right. We needed to follow procedure.

I stood there trying to figure out how I could connect with her. *Hi, Melody,* I said softly.

To my amazement, I felt on some level that she could sense my presence. I could feel her thoughts shift to me, as her soul acknowledged me. I could feel her concern after the conversation she had just had with Detective Cunningham. She sighed as she opened her top desk drawer and pulled out a newspaper clipping. It was a story about my suicide. She studied it. It was as if my presence was enough for her to think about me.

I really need your help, Melody.

She brought Wesley's file up on her computer. She didn't open it, she just sat there and gazed at it. She was in turmoil, and not sure what to do. How could I let her know I was there?

Please, Melody. He's the one who murdered them, I said into her ear. Suddenly, I could feel Detective Cunningham needing me and I allowed his energy to pull me to him.

As I arrived back in his office, he was on his phone.

I'm here, low on energy, I typed. I was so exhausted from communicating, but I knew I had to find a way to find another source of energy.

"Thought you might want to be here," he said out loud, hanging up his phone.

Thank you, I typed. I saw his cell phone sitting by his computer and I touched it, absorbing what energy I could. After I finished, it beeped to let him know it needed to be charged.

"What the...I just charged this." Then, his attention switched back to his ringing office phone.

"Yes, Stacy? Thank you. That's good to hear. Look, I need a favor...I have a Wesley Cavanagh coming in for questioning. I need to make sure that everything is done by the book and all the equipment is working…"

"Yes, interview room four would be perfect. Cameras and audio are in full working order? Perfect, we will be attempting to retrieve a discarded DNA sample. That is the highest priority for this visit. He is a possible murder suspect…"

"Yes. A cold soda or bottled water should work. That would be great, thanks so much Stacy, oh wait…could you also crank up the heat in that room, please? Thank you, Stacy. You're the best."

Detective Cunningham hung up the phone and reviewed the information he had on Riley's case.

"Tallon, I'm hoping to get Wesley on Riley's attempted kidnapping and obtain a DNA sample. Once we have obtained his DNA, I am confident we will have what we need. In addition to comparing it to the facemask and to the DNA samples we obtained from Bryndle's body, Wesley's DNA will also be uploaded into a national database. If he has committed any other crimes and left DNA evidence, we will know about it. I am anxious to get the results back from the ski mask. I know you're low on energy and can't respond but I thought I would let you what my plans are."

A woman stood in his doorway. "I'm sorry, Detective, what did you say?"

"Nothing, Joyce, I'm just talking out loud to myself," he said, laughing.

As she walked away, he shook his head. "Tallon, we are going to need to come up with another plan before rumors regarding my mental health start going around."

Bahahahah, I typed, adding a smiley face.

"Oh, I see your energy is coming back," he said teasingly.

Ann and Michele Modtland

CHAPTER EIGHTEEN

The Art of Interrogation

WAITING OUTSIDE THE INTERVIEW room, Jones and Bradley greeted Detective Cunningham.

"Hello, sir," they said in unison.

"How long has he been waiting?" Cunningham asked.

"Almost two hours," Jones replied.

"Did he give you a hard time about coming in for questioning?"

"Not really, sir. He was pretty cocky, wasn't worried at all. He has been asking when he can leave though, says he needs to get home to take care of his grandmother. From the looks of that house, it doesn't seem like he has taken good care of her. She has a big bruise on her face. In fact, we sent adult protective services to his house after we got him settled in the interrogation room," Bradley said.

"Does he know you sent APS in?"

"No sir," Jones said.

"Good." Detective Cunningham's voice was low as he looked through the one-way mirror at Wesley, who sat relaxed in his chair without an apparent care in the world. "Let's keep that between us for now. Hope he's thirsty."

"Should be, it's awfully warm in there." Jones laughed.

"Perfect."

"Oh, and one more interesting thing to note, sir," Jones added.

"Yes, Jones?"

"When we picked Mr. Cavanaugh up..." Jones looked at Bradley.

"Yes?"

"Well, he's pretty beat up, fresh abrasions and bruises on his body from what we saw. Looks like he's been in a fight. We suggested we could take him to a hospital to be checked out, but he refused."

"Is that right?" Detective Cunningham had a hard time suppressing a smirk.

"Yes. I think Tom, the father from the attack last night, got in a few more good punches than he thought. Because when we asked him about it—"

"Yeah?" Cunningham inquired with amusement.

"He got all defensive about it, says he's fine," Jones finished.

"I'm not so sure Tom had anything to do with it, Jones," Detective Cunningham said with a chuckle.

Jones looked at him inquisitively. "Well, someone kicked his ass. That's all I'm saying."

Detective Cunningham smiled. "My guess is he deserved it."

"No doubt in my mind, sir," Bradley added.

They all chuckled. "Thank you, detectives, good work. Let's go in before he loses his patience with us. No one talks to him but me," Detective Cunningham clarified.

"Sounds good, sir," Jones answered.

All three of them entered the room. The two detectives sat in chairs on opposite ends of the room and Detective Cunningham sat at the table directly across from Wesley.

Wesley's face was swollen. He had two black eyes and butterfly bandages on his right eye, clearly a homemade job.

"Hello. Mr. Cavanagh, my name is Detective Cunningham," he said, shaking Wesley's hand. "How are you doing today?"

"Good, sir, thank you. Please, call me Wesley."

"Okay, Wesley. Sorry to keep you waiting, but it's been a busy day. I sure appreciate you coming in today to answer a few questions."

"Oh, no problem sir, it's the least I can do. Anything I can do to help. I appreciate all the work you people do to keep our community safe. You guys are my heroes," he said, obviously trying to manipulate Detective Cunningham.

"Thank you, Wesley, it's always good to hear that. We take a lot of pride in our work. If you don't mind me asking, what happened to your face? Were you in a fight?"

"Oh no, sir," he said and chuckled. "I'm in training to be a professional mixed martial arts fighter."

I couldn't believe how capable Wesley was of lying on the spot. He turned on the charm for Detective Cunningham. Wesley didn't skip a beat, as he gave details about his fictional training session. Even I may have believed him, had I not known the truth.

"As you can see, I need a little more training," Wesley said, pointing to his face.

Detective Cunningham laughed with him, "I see. Well, Wesley, I have a few questions for you."

"Yes sir, absolutely. I've been wondering what this is all about."

"The reason you have been brought in for questioning today is that there was a home invasion and attempted kidnapping near your neighborhood late last night."

"I can't believe it! Something like that happened in our neighborhood last night. Who would do such a horrible thing? I was just thinking I needed to get an alarm system for our home to keep my grandma safe. Oh, my gosh, she is home alone right now. I'm worried."

"We have police patrolling the area, so I am sure she is okay."

"Thank you, that makes me feel much better, Detective Cunningham."

"Of course, Wesley. We are just talking to people, especially young men who live in that area to see if they heard or saw anything. Did you hear anything around one thirty last night?"

"No sir, I didn't."

"Were you on Maple Street last night around one thirty?"

"No, sir."

"Have you ever been to three four five two Maple Street?"

"No, sir."

"Where were you last night between one and two?"

"I was home with my grandma," Wesley answered in an innocent voice.

"And she can vouch for that?"

"Yes, sir, I was home. I live at my grandma's. She's getting old and has been sick lately. I take care of her and give her medications every night and we watch one of her TV shows together before I help her to bed."

Wesley sounded so sincere and genuine, it made me sick.

"You take care of your grandma? That's very noble of you. Most kids your age would be too busy doing their own thing. I think that's great of you." Detective Cunningham played into his ego.

"She took great care of me, growing up. I love my grandma. She means everything to me. Now it's my turn to care for her, you know what I mean?"

"I can see that. She is lucky to have you." Detective Cunningham continued his supportive questioning technique as Wesley smiled, obviously believing Detective Cunningham thought he was a great person.

"Man, its hot in here," Detective Cunningham said, wiping at his neck. "Can you turn down the heat and get me a drink please?" he asked, motioning to Jones. "Wesley, can I get you a drink? We have juice, water, or soda. What's your drink? Let me guess, water or juice because you are in training, am I right?"

"Yep, water please," Wesley said, smiling. "Thank you, sir."

"Absolutely, Wesley. Okay, it looks like we can get you cleared pretty quickly and get your name off the possible suspect list. Let me just make some notes really quickly."

Jones reentered the room and gave water bottles to Detective Cunningham, Bradley and Wesley. Detective Cunningham opened his and drank from it. Wesley, Bradley, and Jones followed suit.

"Okay, so you have an alibi, your grandmother. Do you care for her every day or just some days?"

"Every day. I train in the morning and then spend the rest of my time at home taking care of her. I clean the house, cook her meals, take her to her doctor appointments, pick up her meds, play bingo with her, get her anything she needs. That's basically my life. Not complaining or anything. I really like being there for her."

I continued to be impressed with his ability to lie and manipulate. I could tell by his interactions and body language that he believed he was smarter than everyone in the room and had no doubt that he was going to get out of this free and clear.

"Okay, that's great. She is sure lucky to have you, Wesley. Let's get this cleared up and get you back home to your grandma. In fact, I'm headed in that direction. How about I drive you home," Detective Cunningham said as Wesley calmly gulped down the rest of the fluid in his water bottle and threw it away in the trash can nearest to them.

"That would be great, detective, thank you."

I followed them out to the parking lot.

"Did you grow up around here, Wesley?"

"Yes sir, born and raised."

"Really? This is a pretty small town, I have a son that is about your age, but I don't remember seeing you around."

"Well, when I was about three, we moved away for a few years. We moved back here when I was seven and my mom got married shortly after. I didn't like her new husband much, so I moved in with grandma. We've been taking care of one another ever since."

"Oh, I see. Did you go to Mount Pine for school then?"

"No sir, I went to a private school."

"A private school here? How did your grandma afford that?"

"Oh, I went to a private school called Pine School Academy, a residential treatment center here. See, when I was twelve, I was having a hard time, and my grandma thankfully decided to get me into treatment while I was young. Best thing that ever happened to me."

"Really? The best thing, huh?"

"Yes sir, that program saved my life. It gave me confidence and taught me to take responsibility for my actions. I hate to think who I would have become today without my experience there."

"That's great. Sounds like it really impacted your life. Pine School Academy, huh? Great school. Has helped so many kids. I have a friend who worked there, back around the time you were there, maybe you know her. Tallon Monroe?"

"No sir, doesn't sound familiar, but if she works there, she must be a great person."

"She actually just passed away recently."

A small smirk flitted across his face. "That's too bad. I'm sorry for your loss. It must be hard to have a friend take their own life. It's a coward's way to go."

I knew what Detective Cunningham was doing. He knew my name would emotionally charge him and perhaps lead him to a slip.

"I didn't say how she died, Wesley."

"Oh, well, sir, it's been all around the news."

"Yes, I suppose it has, but you said the name Tallon Monroe didn't sound familiar to you."

They pulled up to the house. Wesley jumped out. "Thank you so much, Detective Cunningham, I appreciate the ride home."

"Yeah, sure, Wesley. Here's my card. If you hear of anything, think of anything, or want to talk about anything, please don't hesitate to contact me," Detective Cunningham said as he looked directly at Wesley.

"Oh, I will be sure to do that, sir," he said as he slammed the car door.

Detective Cunningham drove back to the police station and sought out Bradley and Jones.

"Did we get the water bottle?" he asked.

"Yes, sir, we did, and we already sent it to the lab for his DNA," Jones said.

"Great job. Thank you. Any word from forensics on the ski mask?"

"It did test positive for blood. It will be a few more days until we get the results back. What did you think about Wesley, sir? Presents as squeaky clean, huh?" Bradley asked.

"I want a tail on him twenty-four hours a day. I don't care what it takes, if you can't cover a shift, call me and I will do it," he ordered Jones and Bradley. "And keep me updated," he added as he shut the door.

"Tallon, are you here, did you hear everything?" he whispered into the air.

Yes, I typed.

"Of course, you did," he said, sitting down at his desk, rubbing his chin with his hand. "I don't like that young man at all, Tallon, not at all. We are going to get him, one way, or another. We are going to get him. I promise you that. For now, it's killing me, but we are just going to have to wait. I pray to God the ski mask will connect him to the attempted child abduction from the other night and to Bryndle's and Oryan's murders. That should be enough to get him off the streets for life."

And if it doesn't? I questioned on the computer screen.

"I don't know, Tallon." He sighed deeply and looked down at his desk, "But we will figure it out. I won't let you down, I promise you that."

CHAPTER NINETEEN

The Gift of Forensics

IT'S THE NOT KNOWING and the waiting that are two of the hardest concepts to cope with in the living domain and even now in death. Waiting? What is time in this realm? It's hard to have a perception of it. I'm sure it was days, maybe even longer, that I remained in the forest with Bryndle. I stayed there in hopes of reaching her and breaking the cycle of her experiencing her murder again and again.

Having no obvious success, and worried that everything was going to rely on the science of forensics, I became withdrawn and emotionally paralyzed. I was distraught about everything that had been revealed to me regarding what Bryndle and Oryan had endured—all because of me. I felt stuck. I felt inadequate. I had no idea how to free Bryndle from this nightmare. It's not as if I didn't try. I let her tell her story and I figured out who the murderer was. I stayed by her side night after night, as her soul tapped into the residual energy left behind by such an atrocious crime. But she was only showing me pieces of the murder. Simultaneously, events were unfolding in the physical world.

As I sat there next to Bryndle, I felt a change in energy around me. As I focused my energy to determine where the change was coming from, I became aware of Detective Cunningham and his urgent call for me.

I shifted back to the police station as I heard Detective Cunningham speaking. "Tallon, where are you?" he called. "Tallon, I don't know where you have been, but I haven't seen or heard from you in weeks, and I have been trying for hours to connect with you. I don't know exactly how this works, but please appear. We got the forensic results back. I think we've got him, Tallon, I think we've got him."

I'm here, catch me up, I typed as fast as I could.

He read the words as they appeared across the screen. "Oh, my God, thank you, Tallon. We found blood splatters on the ski mask and they match Bryndle's DNA. Not only that, but we retrieved Wesley's DNA from the water bottle. It matches the DNA sample that we retrieved from under Bryndle's nails. We're in the process of getting a warrant for his arrest and to search his home. I want the other articles of clothes from the crimes that you told me about. With this evidence, it will be a slam dunk, case closed."

Oh, my God. It worked. We are going to get him. I was overjoyed and excited. The lights in his office glowed even brighter, as some of my excitement escaped into the physical world.

This is great news, Detective Cunningham, thank you. I knew you could do it, I typed.

Detective Bradley stuck her head into the office. "We have the warrant."

Detective Cunningham grabbed his cell phone and gun from his desk. "Let's move out—and stick to the plan as I briefed you this morning. I want everything done by the book."

About a dozen officers and detectives gathered their gear and moved out. As they left, I warped to Wesley's house. He was sitting on the couch watching television and drinking a beer. No real surprise there. *You are so arrogant, Wesley. You can't even comprehend what is about to happen. This is retribution for everything you did to Bryndle's and Oryan.* I looked around the house and saw no sign of his grandmother. *Thank goodness,* I whispered. *Grandma doesn't need to witness anything more.*

I watched as the SWAT team silently approached the house. Police cars had every inch of the street covered. Some of the police officers had armed themselves and barricaded themselves behind their opened car doors, while Detective Cunningham and two SWAT officers knocked on the front door. Wesley got up from the couch and peeked through the blinds to see his house surrounded by police. This shocked Wesley initially, but he managed to convince himself he still had control of the situation. He calmly opened the front door.

"How can I help you, gentlemen?"

"Wesley Cavanaugh, you are under arrest for the murder of Bryndle Monroe and her unborn child and for the attempted kidnapping of Riley Smith," Detective Cunningham announced, grabbing Wesley's arms and turning him against the wall to handcuff his hands behind his back.

"You have the right to remain silent. Anything you say, can and will be used against you in a court of law. You have the right to talk to an attorney and to have an attorney present with you while you are being questioned. If you cannot afford to hire an attorney, one will be appointed to represent you, if you wish. You can decide at any time to exercise these rights and not answer any questions or make any statements. Do you understand each of these rights as I have explained them to you? Having these rights in mind, do you wish to talk to us now?" Detective Cunningham spoke with authority as he walked Wesley to a police car.

"Yes, sir, but this is a big mistake, sir. I will help you get this figured out in any way I can," Wesley said confidently.

Detective Cunningham ignored Wesley's comment as he pressed his hand on Wesley's head to guide him into the back seat of the police car. Wesley turned his head to look at Detective Cunningham. "This is a mistake, Detective. I would never hurt anyone."

Again, Cunningham ignored him. "Officers, you can take him in, thanks." He shut the door and rapped on the car's roof, and the squad car pulled away.

Detective Cunningham then walked to his forensic team, dressed in white coveralls with paper booties covering their shoes. "All right, let's be thorough about this. I don't want anything missed. Take your time. I have arranged for food and drinks to be delivered. Anything else you need, let me know. I'm here to support you in any way I can. I know you don't need to be reminded that this a murder investigation, and you are the best of the best. We've been informed there is possible evidence located under his bed. We're looking for a box containing clothes that may have been worn during the murder. Let me know when you have recovered the box, along with any other evidence you can find."

Hours passed. I waited outside under a tent with Detective Cunningham, not wanting to interfere with the search. Media vans were beginning to pull up, and the street was filled with spectators. A helicopter circled above, as other media filmed the scene below. The forensic team had set tents up everywhere to block the helicopter's view. Officers guarded the area they had outlined in yellow tape. Periodically, the forensics team brought out sealed and marked bags and put them in their van. The lead forensic specialist approached Detective Cunningham.

"Sir, there was nothing under the bed, and we have concluded our investigation. We didn't find the box of clothes you were referring to. I have my team doing an additional sweep of the property to see if we could have missed anything. We have been through every inch of the house three times and we will keep looking if you wish."

What? No, no! Wesley didn't know the detectives were on to him and those items meant too much for him to get rid of them. There is no way, he wouldn't have disposed of the clothing. No, I don't believe it! I shouted, even though no one could hear me.

"It has to be there somewhere. I tried to get the bloodhounds from Charleston, but they were on another case today," Detective Cunningham said, pacing impatiently in front of the team. "Can I get a clean forensics outfit? I want to look for myself. We'll go through the house one more time tonight before it gets dark. If we are unable to find the box, we'll get the dogs here tomorrow."

"That sounds like a plan. Let me get you suited up," the forensic leader said, walking away.

I noticed someone catch Detective Cunningham's attention, and he walked toward the group of people gathered beyond the yellow tape. It was my dad, his arms folded as he intently watched the investigation.

"Arthur, you shouldn't be here," Detective Cunningham told my dad sympathetically.

"Did you get him? I saw something on the news. Is it true?"

"Arthur." Detective Cunningham paused for a moment, knowing he could be heard by others in the crowd. He pulled my dad close. "We got him," he whispered. "I am sorry you heard about it from the news. It should not have been released yet that way. I was planning on heading to your house right after we finished."

Tears slipped down my dad's cheeks. I wanted so badly to hug and comfort him.

"You need to be home with your family. I'll let you know as soon as we're done. But now I will have an officer give you a ride home," Detective Cunningham said.

"It's okay, Detective Cunningham. My car is just around the corner," my dad interrupted. He continued to cry, something I had rarely seen him do. He looked so heartbroken. "I can get myself home. I just miss my girls so much and they deserve justice."

"Are you sure you'll be okay? I'll send officers home with you to help with any media that might be there."

"I'm sure. And thank you, Detective Cunningham."

My dad turned and walked into the crowd. I wanted to follow him, but I knew I needed to stay here.

"We have your suit ready, sir," the lead forensic specialist said, walking up to Detective Cunningham. "If you want to head to the orange tent, my colleague will help you in dressing...whenever you're ready."

"Thanks," Detective Cunningham said as he made a quick call on his cell phone. "Can you send additional officers to the Monroe house to block off the media? Yes, that's fine. Thank you."

Minutes later, Detective Cunningham, fully clothed in white forensic coveralls, entered the house again along with the forensic team.

I watched in frustration as they searched every room, to no avail. I remembered the way he had fondled that box, caressing each article of clothing, smelling each item as if to savor a memory, and carefully laying each item out on his bed. These were his souvenirs. There is no way he would have discarded them. *Perhaps he moved the box to a safer location,* I thought, so I concentrated on the box, envisioning it in my mind and searching for the energy it contained, hoping I could sense its present location. I identified a murky, sad energy projecting from behind the headboard of Wesley's bed. I stuck my head through the wall, and there it was. He had hollowed out a section of the wall and carefully covered the hole with wallpaper so no one could see his hiding spot. Wesley must have wanted to keep the clothing close to him when he slept. I just knew he couldn't part with his souvenirs.

As everyone exited the bedroom, I knew I needed to alert Detective Cunningham to Wesley's hiding place. Using my energy, I quickly turned the lights off and on a couple of times.

"Hmmm, there must be a short," the lead forensic specialist said.

"Must be," Detective Cunningham said. "Or it's haunted." They both chuckled.

"I'll check the breaker...assuming it's not haunted," the lead forensic specialist laughed, as she left the room.

He knew it was me, and I sent him a cool breeze to validate my presence.

"Okay, what are you trying to tell me, Tallon?" He looked around to make sure no one was observing.

I turned on the lamp next to the bed. Detective Cunningham looked around and then moved the bed back from the wall. He got down on his knees to look at the floorboards. He put his left hand on the wallpapered wall for stability and felt a gap in the wall where his thumb rested. He felt around the wall with both hands.

"There's a hole in the wall under this wallpaper," he said, yelling for his team. "Hey, I think I've got something!"

Two forensic team members reentered the bedroom.

"What is it, sir?" one of them asked.

"There is a hollow area, here behind the wallpaper."

The forensic team carefully cut away the wallpaper to reveal a hole, just large enough to fit the hat box.

"There's a box hidden in here," one of the forensic team members said, pulling the box out of the wall and carefully placing it on the floor.

Detective Cunningham lifted the lid and saw the articles of black clothing folded neatly inside. "This is what we were looking for. Put all this in an evidence bag. And I want this bag analyzed, first thing. We got him. After all these years, we finally got him."

CHAPTER TWENTY

The Murder

AS I SAT ON my bench in the forest clearing, I felt profound relief, knowing Wesley could no longer harm another human being. I was overcome with gratitude for all those who had trusted me and helped me bring him to justice in the right way. *Thank you,* I cried to the universe. Now I could focus solely on helping Bryndle.

I walked to the pine tree and leaned against it. I could feel the life in it and the secrets it held.

Bryndle, honey, we got Wesley Cavanagh. He will never hurt anyone again. I want you to know I'm here, and I'm trying to figure out how to help you. I could feel her spirit pulling me and allowed myself to be taken.

I found myself at work in my office. I stood next to the window and noticed snow was falling. I watched my past self, sitting at my desk, talking on the phone. As I listened, I remembered this conversation. It was the last time I had talked with Bryndle. My heart sank. How I wished I could change that night. I should have been with her.

I had called Bryndle from work about eight thirty that evening. I was supposed to take her out for Chinese food and ice cream, to satisfy her latest cravings, but an issue had come up at work. Something always seemed to come up at work. I told her I wasn't going to be able to make it and promised her that I would make it up to her later. I remember her words exactly, as I have replayed them again and again in my mind.

"It's okay, babe, I understand. Emergencies come up. My feet are so swollen though, I think I am going to go out quickly to buy a new pair of shoes. Maybe some ugly slippers or something that will fit on my feet and help me get some relief. I know you think slippers are incredibly sexy," she joked, laughing.

"You can make anything look sexy, honey," I responded, teasing.

"Oh, whatever. I am pregnant with your child and I feel like a giant balloon about to pop. I'm anything but sexy," she said, laughing again. "I should be home before you, so let me know if you are hungry, and want me to stop and get something for you."

"Okay, honey, sounds good. I love you, drive safe."

"I love you, too, sweetheart."

God, I missed her, the sound of her voice, her laughter. I couldn't help but tear up as I heard our playful conversation.

Suddenly, I was pulled to our house. Bryndle was hanging up the phone. She waddled around the house, her feet swollen, barely fitting into her flip flops, the only shoes she could get on her feet now. I loved seeing her like this again. She grabbed her keys and put Chewy in the kitchen.

"I'll be right back, boy."

Chewy whined.

"I know, baby, but it's too cold for you to come with me tonight. I won't be long, I promise. When I get home, I will make you some popcorn, okay?" Bryndle leaned and kissed his head. "I love you. I'll be right back."

Chewy let out another small whine.

I watched as she left her red coat behind—she was always so hot in her last trimester—and drove to the shopping center. Bryndle parked her ancient but prized nineteen seventy-four red Ford Galaxy five hundred, the last model ever made, on the right side of the store, which happened to be the darkest side. In hindsight, it probably wasn't the smartest move. Because of the confusion her pregnancy sometimes caused, she often forgot where she parked. She parked on the right side of every building, in the same spot every time, so she would never forget where her car was. I couldn't help but realize how easy we made this for Wesley, how her predictability was dangerous. I watched as she slowly made her way into the store, choosing her steps carefully in the snow as she walked in her flip-flops. And then I saw him. He came out of the shadows at the back of the store. He knew she would park there. he had been watching her, probably since he was discharged from the treatment facility in Idaho. He was just waiting for the right opportunity, for her to show up alone at night. He stood there by our car watching her walk up to the store.

As she walked, Bryndle saw Elliot.

"Hi, Elliot, how are you tonight?"

"Good, how are you, Mrs. Monroe?"

"Oh, I'm struggling a little bit. My feet are so swollen. They are probably even bigger than yours," she joked.

They compared feet, and I realized this is when she got his shoe size. I couldn't help but smile at the beautiful person my wife was as I watched them talk. Bryndle finally said goodbye to Elliot and went directly into the shoe department where she picked out slippers for herself and new shoes for Elliot. Then she went into the grocery section for some food she planned to cook for dinner. On her way out, she went out of her way to run into Elliot again. As she gave him the shoes, I saw Wesley slip into the back seat of our car where he hid as Bryndle approached. Watching this was so difficult. I would do anything to be able to intervene. But that was not possible. As she pulled out of the parking lot Wesley popped up from the back seat and held a gun to her head.

"Drive straight. I'll tell you when to pull over. Do as I say and don't talk. If you listen to me, you might not get hurt."

"Please, don't hurt me, I'll do whatever you want. Please, I'm pregnant," she said, her voice shaking. She put the car in gear, but the car swerved as she tried to look at him in the rear-view mirror.

He shoved the gun harder into her cheek and pushed her head forward. "Keep your eyes on the road, lady. Drive straight, and not too fast." Wesley tightly grabbed a chunk of her long blond hair in his fist and yanked her head. "Slow down!"

Bryndle was terrified. She was trembling, not sure what to do. They didn't drive far. The clearing was only five, maybe ten minutes from the shopping center.

"Pull over...there behind the trees. Right next to that car."

It was his car. He must have left his car at the clearing days before. He had been hunting Bryndle and planning this night for weeks.

"Turn the ignition off and give me the keys."

She turned the car off and handed him the keys. He got out of the backseat and moved to Bryndle's door. She quickly locked the car doors, not realizing that he had left the back door ajar. He jumped back into the car and reached into the front to pistol whip her with his gun. The blow knocked her out and when she came to, she was lying on the snow-covered ground in the clearing. He was on top of her, trying to pull her shirt off. She managed to grab a rock she felt near her and hit him across the face. As he fell back, Bryndle struggled to her feet and ran, losing her flip flops, running barefoot in the snow. It only took him a few seconds to get back up and chase after her.

Bryndle screamed for help and ran as fast as she could, but she was slowed by the awkwardness of her pregnancy. Unfortunately, she could only flee deeper into the woods. He quickly caught up with her and tackled her to the ground. Then he began hitting her in the face. She tried to block the blows with her arms, but her attempts to defend herself were futile. He laughed as she fought back. Somehow, she again got away and stumbled along the path by the river. She tripped and as she tried to recover from her fall, Wesley reached her, pulled out a knife and plunged it toward her distended stomach. She defended her belly—our baby—with her hands and then rolled as he stabbed at her repeatedly.

She begged for him to stop, and to please spare her baby. This encouraged his brutality even more. As they fought, she knocked the knife out of his hands with her elbow, got to her feet and tried to run again as he searched for the knife in the snow. Her flight was to no avail and she fell again, weakened with the loss of so much blood. She faded in and out of consciousness as she lay there bleeding to death next to the river.

Wesley finally found the knife and, taking note of her location, calmly walked to his car parked among the trees near the forest clearing. As he retrieved a satchel from his car and walked back to Bryndle, she regained consciousness and struggled onto her hands and knees. She started crawling while holding her belly, barely able to see through her swollen eyes. She desperately tried to feel her way across the broken, frozen ground with what was left of her badly damaged hands. Bryndle possessed an incredible amount of strength and courage, but because it took everything she had to concentrate on getting away, she didn't hear Wesley approach. Without warning, he kicked her in the face so hard that it flipped her whole body over. I gasped as I realized that her face was so swollen and bleeding so badly that she was unrecognizable. She choked on her own blood, as he stood above her and just laughed. He gazed coldly at her, as if he were taking in every detail of her mangled and bloody body. Then he took a gas can out of the satchel and poured gasoline on her.

No, please no! I found myself pleading out loud as the smell of the gas masked the normal smell of the surrounding pines.

As I realized what was going to happen next, it broke my heart as I heard my wife cry out. "God, please help me! Please, just save my baby." But her cries were unanswered.

He lit the match and dropped it on my beloved's body. She screamed in agony and let out an unearthly cry as she died. Wesley watched with a satisfied grin as her body went up in flames. I watched in horror as her soul left her body. As for Wesley, he just calmly walked through the trees, got into his car, and drove away.

I stood there paralyzed by what I had just witnessed. Although I had seen glimpses of this malicious attack, I had never seen the whole event play out before my eyes. Now I knew the full horror my beloved wife had endured. I dropped to my knees, next to her body and instinctively tried to roll her body to put the fire out. I felt responsible for what she had suffered. I held her close and cried.

I am so sorry Bryndle, I am so sorry. This is all my fault. I'm so sorry, Bryndle. I am so sorry, I said as I sobbed uncontrollably. Finally, I allowed my love to surround both of us, dissolving all my anger, guilt, and regret. I saw things I had been unwilling to see before. I saw the strands of energy that tied her to Wesley, to the pain of the memory, and the fear of losing our baby. My love continued to expand until all that was left was love and acceptance for what I had been unable to fully understand. Her body disappeared in the light of that love and I feared I still hadn't been able to save her. I sat silently, not sure what to do next.

Tallon? Bryndle's voice called to me softly. *Tallon, is that you?* I turned slowly wondering if her voice was just in my head.

Bryndle? I jumped to my feet. *Bryndle, honey?*

She stood before me, still manifesting the injuries that her body had endured.

Tallon, I can't feel the baby! Bryndle wept as she looked at her life-ending injuries and fell to her knees. *I'm sorry, Tallon. I tried to save our baby. I tried so hard.*

I put my arms around her and rocked her.

Everything is okay, my love. It's finished now. The baby is okay. You're okay. We're all okay, honey. It's over. You're safe now. I could feel a new pure, powerful love growing inside me.

Still tied to the horror around us and in a state of shock, she remained confused and cried inconsolably. We just held one another and we both cried. This new powerful love I had uncovered surrounded Bryndle as well. I closed my eyes and envisioned Bryndle healthy and whole, and begged her to accept my healing love, to allow herself to believe everything was okay—to trust me. Slowly, she healed. As I identified the residual energy that was binding Bryndle to the scene of her murder, I was able to cut her ties to Wesley, the murder, the fear, and all the emotions keeping her there. She shone with a white light. I was overcome with joy—my beautiful wife, who had endured what no one should, was standing before me whole, something I feared I would never see again.

I can't believe it. You're really here. I'm never letting you go again, I cried.

I'm dead, aren't I? Bryndle asked me.

I nodded, unable to vocalize the words.

Then how can I feel you? She looked around and stood up. *Why are you here, Tallon?* She covered her mouth. *Oh, my God, Tallon are you…?* She pointed at me.

Yes, Bryndle.

What happened? she said in panic. *I thought you said our baby was okay.* She paused. *Where is the baby?*

Oryan is fine, she is with your parents and my grandma.

White light filled the clearing and surrounded us. I could sense that Bryndle realized we were dead but was not aware of all that had happened. Several people approached us from within the light.

My parents, oh, my God, Tallon, it's my mom and dad. She looked at me smiling, as she ran toward them. She embraced them and held on tight. Her mom motioned to my grandma who was holding our beautiful baby girl. Bryndle stared at her in disbelief, crying as my grandma gently handed Oryan to her.

She's perfect, Tallon. Look at her.

I know. She has your eyes, I said, as I held them both.

Oryan. Oh, my gosh, I love you so much, baby girl, Bryndle whispered.

I couldn't stop looking at my incredible family. My wife, my daughter, my grandmother, and my in-laws—all here with me. I felt so blessed for us all to be together. Then Michael approached and greeted Bryndle.

Hello Bryndle. My name is Michael. I see you have all been reunited. Welcome home, he said with a warm and loving smile. *I am deeply sorry you had to endure such a horrific passing. I want you to know that your cries did not go unheard, that we sent an army of angels to comfort you. Unfortunately, we are unable to intervene with the choices of others. We can send angels to guide their choices toward love but, ultimately, the decision is theirs. In the end, all we can do is love you and support you. All of heaven cried with you, my beloved, and we all stood amazed at your valiant fight to save not only your life but the life of your child.* A tear slipped down Michael's face as he turned to address me.

Tallon. You've shown great perseverance, dedication, and strength, he said as his voice cracked. *Tallon, this is a complex situation and one that I have never encountered before. Your choices were made in love and selflessness. Nevertheless, as we discussed before, you are responsible for the consequences of your actions, no matter the intent. Bryndle and Oryan's lives were taken by an act of evil. You, however, chose to take your own life and turned away from the light.*

Tallon, what have you done? Bryndle interrupted. Michael motioned for her to let him speak.

We all have contracts or promises we make in life and we have a responsibility to keep them to the best of our ability. By taking your life, you made it more difficult to keep those contracts and you will need to do your best to make amends for them without a physical body. Unfortunately, you are not ready to come to the light until you have made amends for your suicide.

What? I did what I had to do to help my wife, I insisted. *I had to.*

Tallon. You have accomplished what you wanted to do. Your wife and daughter are safe now. Is that not what you wanted?

Yes.

What is your inner voice, your higher self telling you, Tallon? Michael asked.

It says there is truth in what you are saying. But I want to be with my family, I insisted.

This isn't easy for me either, Tallon. As I said before, I have never encountered this situation. However, once you have taken your life, you have to repair the damage you caused to the best of your ability. We can't make exceptions, no matter the intent behind the act. Furthermore, it's my responsibility to nurture you, as long ago I made a promise to you to help you grow and realize your full abilities.

I understand, I said to Michael, but in all reality, I was devastated. All I had wanted, all I had done, was because I wanted Bryndle to be safe and for us to be reunited as a family. I had never considered that I wouldn't be able to be with them. How could I say goodbye?

Trying not to cry, I turned to look at my wife. *I'm so sorry, Bryndle.*

Sorry? she said as she tried to understand the situation. *You don't have to be sorry—you gave up everything to save me,* she said as tears ran down her face. *All I can say is, thank you, Tallon. I can't believe you did that for me. I'm the one who should be saying sorry.*

I gently cut her off. *You and Oryan are safe now and that is all that matters. I won't be gone long. I will figure this out, honey, and we will be together soon.*

I choked back my tears. I didn't want her to worry about me.

I will always be here, Tallon, waiting for you.

It's time, Tallon, Michael said.

I hugged and kissed Bryndle goodbye and told my baby girl I would be back soon. I hugged my grandma and my in-laws and thanked them for taking such good care of Oryan, and then I stood there and watched my family as they disappeared into the light.

I wept, but I knew that everything Michael had said was true—that in taking my life I had inadvertently changed the course of other souls' paths and now I needed to go back and fix it with the knowledge that Bryndle and Oryan were safe, I could now go back and freeheartedly fix the pain I had caused to all the souls I had left behind.

CHAPTER TWENTY-ONE

The Beginning of Redemption

LEFT ALONE, I SAT on the bench, taking an emotional inventory of my present state. In doing so, I came to the realization that I could do one of two things. I could either wallow in self-pity, not rectifying anything—which would only keep me ostracized from my wife and baby, or I could take responsibility for my actions that had stunted my spiritual growth. If I took the latter path, I had to figure out what I needed to do to make amends for my suicide.

I'm not going to lie. I was lonely to the core, longing for my family. But, for the first time since the murder, I experienced a peace inside me, a stillness, knowing my wife and daughter were finally safe and happy and where they belonged—the two of them together, residing in a place where no one could harm them ever again, where they were receiving love from my grandma and Bryndle's parents and many others. How could I be sad about that? I couldn't. It's all I ever wanted for them—to be safe, happy, and surrounded by an abundance of love. This was a reality that never could have manifested if I had chosen to remain living on earth. So, in truth, I had no regrets for what I had done. Sunlight reached my face through the pine trees' boughs. I closed my eyes as I lifted my face and truly felt the sun. In that moment, I was confident I would be all right. Regardless of what was next, I would be fine. My loved ones were safe.

I stood up. I had no regrets. I would do it again to save Bryndle, so I needed to stop acting like a victim, and I needed to take responsibility for what I had done and fix what I could. I proclaimed this to the universe. Although I was ready to move forward, I stood there perplexed for a moment. I wondered to myself, how do I repair something I couldn't take back? What redemption, as Michael called it, did I need to complete? How do I figure out what I should do? It all seemed so complex, yet I was lighter, freer than I had ever been. The constant worry and desperation to help Bryndle was gone. *I can do this*, I told myself.

I decided to visit my parents first. It felt like the place to go for clarity. It had been some time since my death now, and I was happy to see that they had embraced my house as their own, just as I had asked them to do in my will. The layout of my house was more spacious and livable for the three of them, and I wasn't surprised at all to see that they had used the bulk of the money I had left them to make it a wheelchair- accessible environment for Odin, making it easier for him to move around.

It looked as if my parents were hosting a family get-together. I used to love my parents' parties. My Aunt Sally, Cecilia, along with her husband and their adorable baby boy, and, to my surprise, Detective Cunningham were all in the front room. The blinds were all shut because media vans were still parked out front.

"Come here, come and see me. Aunt Rose wants to kiss those adorable cheeks," I heard my mom call out as she picked up Cecilia's baby boy from the floor. He was crawling now. "Tallon, Aunt Rose got you ice cream," she said as she smiled at him.

What? They named the baby after me? I said, putting my hands to my heart.

"He is adorable, and what a great name," Detective Cunningham said warmly.

"It is the perfect name. Tallon is really the only reason we both made it. It's a long story, but I believe Tallon still watches over us, and I wanted her to know she will always be a member of this family," Cecilia explained.

"I'm sure that means a lot to her, and I think you are right. Tallon is watching out for the ones she loves," Detective Cunningham agreed.

My mother looked right at Detective Cunningham as if picking up on the emotion and deeper meaning of his words. Detective Cunningham looked down and cleared his throat.

"I apologize for the intrusion," he said. "I stopped by to personally inform you we arrested a young man this morning by the name of Wesley Cavanaugh for the murders of Bryndle and her unborn child. I understand the news has been reporting a possible connection to your case. I'm sorry I couldn't get here sooner, but arresting Mr. Cavanagh was top priority."

"We understand, Detective," my dad said.

How thoughtful for him to reach out to my family. I watched his body language as he explained everything that had transpired. I had so much love and respect for this man. He also seemed lighter. He had a spark in his eyes and his shoulders were no longer slumped. I was touched to see my dad move closer to my mom to hold her hand as they listened to every word Detective Cunningham had to say.

He explained to my parents that Wesley was once a resident at the adolescent treatment facility where I had worked. Detective Cunningham relayed some of Wesley's history to my parents, mentioning the incident between Wesley and me at the facility years ago.

"I remember that. I tried so hard to get Tallon to press charges, but she believed everyone deserves a second chance. She wouldn't give up on anyone. That's just our loving girl," my dad said as he choked up.

"How did you figure it out, after all this time?" my mother asked.

Detective Cunningham looked down and then spoke nervously but honestly. "Well, I don't mean to alarm you, but I'm not sure you will even believe me. This definitely needs to stay between us." He took a deep breath. "Tallon helped me from the other side. If you ask me, I think that's why she did it, you know to…"

My mother nodded in acknowledgment.

The room went quiet and Cecilia was the first to speak. "I believe it. Of course, she did. I believe you."

"What do you mean exactly that she helped you from the other side? How?" my mother asked, clutching at my dad's hand.

As Detective Cunningham tried his best to relay the details of how everything had unfolded, Chewy and Odin came into the room. Chewy came right up to me and started wagging his tail. He saw me! I knelt and told him how much I loved him. I asked him to take care of the family, and I told him that his mom and Oryan were safe. I looked up only to see Odin watching our interaction. He had a big smile. I stood up, tilted my head to the side and watched his eyes follow. I smiled lovingly at him and signed *I love you, buddy*. Enthusiastically, he bounced up and down in his wheelchair and squealed. "I love you, too, Tallon."

Everyone turned to watch Chewy and Odin's excitement.

"Would you look at that," my father said in bewilderment as he pointed at Chewy's wagging tail and pricked ears focused on something or someone no one else could see.

"What did you say, honey?" my mother asked Odin.

"I'm telling Tallon I love her, too," Odin replied.

"Is she here, honey?"

"She's right there, Mom."

Everyone looked in my direction. "Tallon, honey if you are here," my mother paused, overcome with emotion, "Please know we love you so much and we are so proud of you. We understand, honey. I understand."

"So proud of you, Tallon, so proud...love and miss you so much," my father added.

Detective Cunningham nodded in approval.

I missed my family. I wanted to give them all a big hug and apologize for all the pain I had caused them. Hearing my mother say she understood meant the world to me. I wanted to share with them everything that I had experienced and everything I still needed to do—to seek their guidance—but I couldn't. There would be no way to convey all of that, but I needed to seize the moment to let them know how much I loved them all.

I spoke to Odin, instead. *Buddy, please tell them that I love them all so much and will always watch out for them.* My heart filled with so many competing emotions as I heard him relay the message to my family. I was thankful Odin and Chewy had been able to see me. I bent down to pet Chewy goodbye and I blew Odin a kiss.

Returning to my bench in the forest, I reviewed everything that had transpired. My family was in a good place now, all because of Detective Cunningham, Odin, and Chewy. What else did I need to do? Who else did I need to connect with, or help, before I could get back with my wife and baby? I wondered. I was so unsure of the answers or where to begin. How do I keep spiritual contracts when I don't have a clear understanding as to what they are? I guess that's the point. I must discover the answers for myself. I thought about the people who may have been affected by my suicide. Obviously, that would include my family and close friends.

Emi! I couldn't believe I had been so forgetful. What about Emi?

I focused on Emi and found her in her loft. It was in disarray, even worse than normal. Emi lay half naked on the couch, the surrounding floor littered with empty beer cans. What is she doing? I thought. I knew Emi wasn't close to her family, but she was close to mine. I thought she would have reached out to them. I heard someone slide a piece of paper under her door. It was an eviction notice. Things were much worse than I would have ever imagined. I could sense the pain in her heart. She was lonely, broken, and needed help.

Emi. Can you hear me? I whispered in her ear. She was motionless. I went to sit on the coffee table to talk to her, when I discovered it was covered in photos of Emi, Bryndle, and myself. There was a note pad next to the pictures in Emi's handwriting. There was a title across the top of the page. "A List of Ways I Could Have Prevented Tallon's Suicide." What had I done to Emi? Of course, she felt responsible! She was my life-long, best friend. I would have felt the same way if the tables had been turned. This wasn't her fault. I had needed to die to save Bryndle.

Emi, I'm sorry, I whispered. *I'm okay, and you will be okay too. You are strong, Emi, and so loved.* I began slowly gliding my hands across her sleeping body to surround her in love and light. I knew I had to get Emi help—and fast. Knowing Emi, I knew she had always searched for a place to belong. I had become her place. We were like family and now she was all alone. She had always been close to my family, and my parents loved her like one of their own, but it wasn't the same. I thought they would have been in better touch, but I imagined Emi had shut herself off like she always did when confronted by pain.

I decided the best way to help Emi was to get Mom involved. I needed someone to help who loved her in the physical world. I focused on my mom and found her lying in bed next to my dad. Perhaps I should have been a little apprehensive after my past experience with Wesley, but this was my mom and I had no fear. I entered her mind to participate in her dream.

Hi Mom! Yes, it's me. I have so many things that I want to say, Mom. I am so sorry for all the pain I caused you and our family, but I had to help Bryndle. Please forgive me. I want you to know how much I love you. You have been the most amazing mother. I feel so blessed to have you and Dad as parents. My childhood was magical, and you've always been there for me. And right now, Mom, I really need help again. I am concerned about Emi.

I put images in her mind of Emi's emotional state and shared my worries with her. I hoped and prayed that I could make a big enough impression on her subconscious that she would remember or at least think she needed to check on Emi. My mother stirred and as her eyes opened, I was pushed out of her mind. I watched as she woke up my dad.

"Arthur, I just had a really bad dream about Emi, I think Tallon just spoke to me in my dreams. She told me Emi was in dark place and needed us. I can't shake this worried feeling, Arthur."

"Well, it sounds like we should reach out to Emi immediately," my dad said. "Let's go see her first thing in the morning."

I love my parents. They are incredible people. I have always been able to count on them in life and now, even in death.

Ann and Michele Modtland

CHAPTER TWENTY-TWO

River

THE BENCH REMAINED MY go to place. I felt comfortable there. I sat admiring the way the moonlight changed everything, and I enjoyed listening to the sound of owls hooting in the night. I marveled at how the trees danced with the wind so intimately. I had never noticed how alive everything was before, how connected it all was. We live in such a beautiful world.

I missed my wife. I missed holding her as we watched television. I missed her smell, her laugh, her touch. I missed everything about her, and I couldn't help but wonder what Oryan was doing. Had she grown? Wait, could she grow in heaven? Was she smiling yet? I had so many questions. I longed to be with them. But I also reminded myself that I got exactly what I wanted. They were safe, and I was blessed to have that knowledge.

I sought to make them proud, and I contemplated what my next step would be after my parents reached out to Emi, when, suddenly, a strange thing happened. I could feel a spirit pulling me. I didn't recognize the energy but suspected I needed to find out what this was. I allowed the spirit to call me.

I was taken to a dilapidated, run-down shed that stood behind an old abandoned house. The property was in horrible condition and looked like it should be condemned. It was dark, and the wind whistled with a low, eerie sound as it blew between gaps in the shed walls. Everything about the setting seemed sad. Lonely. The trees surrounding the property were bare of leaves and the ground was frozen. Everything was dark and deprived of color—it was an environment clearly suffering from the absence of attention and love.

I could sense a soul in the shed but was hesitant to enter. Unfamiliar with my surroundings and this strange energy, I was alert and cautious. The shed seemed unstable as it shook and creaked when I slipped through the door. Chips of yellowed white paint fell from the door jamb and onto the floorboards, leaving the impression more of a sealed tomb than a dirty, weather-worn woodshed.

As I entered, I saw some movement in a back corner. I stepped forward and saw an African American woman huddled against the wall and holding her knees as she rocked herself back and forth. I moved closer and realized she was wearing lightweight pajamas and had no shoes or socks on her feet.

I checked the shed to make sure we were alone and then watched her for a few moments, trying to decide what to do. She didn't appear to be from the living world. *Hello,* I said tentatively, but she didn't respond. Not sure if I was reading the situation correctly, I spoke again. *My name is Tallon, and I am here to help you. Is everything okay?*

She turned her head toward me. I gave her a reassuring smile, and she screamed out loud in an inhuman way that distorted her face. She appeared to have fangs and her eyes were bulging out of her head. I took a few panicky steps back and tripped on a bucket. I lay frozen on the ground, frightened. *What the hell was this?* I asked myself.

Leave now! she growled as she slithered toward me.

I jumped to my feet and slowly backed out of the shed, keeping my eyes on her the whole time. *What was that? What is this? Why am I here?* I fretted. I felt a darkness and an unfamiliar pain. I wanted to leave, but I knew I was there for a reason. I thought through all my options and then I wondered if surrounding her in white light would help her.

I entered the shed again. Terrified that she would be upset, I found myself trembling. I closed my eyes, an action difficult to do when you are petrified, and I called upon love and light. She was aware of my presence, but unreceptive to the help I was offering. I opened my eyes again to find her angry face inches away from mine. I shrieked. She grew large, doubling in size as she tried to intimidate me into leaving. My error was in letting her see my fear. I stood my ground and called back the love and light I had released in the shed. She became small again, human-sized. She walked to the corner to curl up and resume rocking herself.

I'm here to help you, I said. *Can you tell me your name?*

She just looked at me with an overwhelming feeling of hopelessness. She cried and wiped her nose on the sleeve of her pajama top. She was an older woman, perhaps in her late sixties, but from her mannerisms she seemed much younger.

Everything is going to be okay. I am here to help, I told her.

She shook her head from side to side in denial.

I thought to myself that maybe I shouldn't be telling her it's going to be fine when I didn't have all the facts as to why she was here. I needed to try a new tactic.

Can you tell me what happened? I asked.

She shook her head and continued to sob.

I took a few steps closer. *Okay, I will just sit here until you are ready.* I sat down a few feet away from her. Her energy made me feel sick and shaky. I surrounded myself in white light to protect myself from her negative energy. I sat there with her for days. She finally turned to me.

You don't give up, do you?

Not on people, no, I declared.

She hung her head down low. *My baby,* she said. *I can't find my baby.*

My eyes widened as I heard the despair in her words, and my heart broke for her. *She's lost her baby,* I thought to myself, and in the next moment I was standing inside the abandoned house. It was as if it had been waiting for me—forsaken, yet full of life with stories to share. The windows were boarded up, and cobwebs hung from the ceiling. There was nothing inside the kitchen, no furniture, no dishes except for an old cup that sat in the sink. I walked around the main level but didn't see anything of great importance until I neared the stairs—something beckoned to me to climb them. I went up slowly. This was different from the experience I had had with Bryndle. I felt unsure of everything. As I climbed the stairs, I was pulled to a small room immediately to the right. I walked inside and could sense a soul. It felt like a child's innocent soul, but I couldn't see anyone. Then the room transformed into a younger version and two beds appeared.

I must be in the past, I thought as I looked around the room. The beds were unmade, the hardwood floors covered in dirt. The entire room was disheveled. Then I heard someone enter the front door. I walked down the stairs to see who it was. A cute, little African-American boy with an afro walked through the door. Judging by his clothing, the time appeared to be in the early seventies or late sixties.

A grown man met him at the base of the stairs. He was in a white T-shirt and ripped jeans, holding a cigarette. I assumed he must be the father.

"Where's River?" the man questioned. The boy looked at him, confused.

"Hello, stupid! Can you hear me?" he said to the little boy as he slapped him on the side of the head. I gasped. How could he treat his son like this?

"Where is your brother?" the father asked again, his tone harsh.

"I...I...I d...d...d"

"I, I, I." He teased him. "I'm stupid," the man said as he laughed, taunting the boy.

I could feel the young boy's tortured soul. The amount of pain this little soul held was almost more than I could bear. *I love you. I am here for you. You are not alone,* I said to him even though I knew he couldn't hear me, but I was hoping he could feel it.

Then, just like that, I was taken farther back in time. I saw a mother yelling at a young teenage girl. The girl looked familiar, and then I recognized her. She was the woman from the shed, the woman missing her baby.

"You always make men leave!" her mother yelled at the crying twelve or thirteen-year-old girl.

"But Mama, he was hurting me."

I believed she was telling the truth and I could sense the pain I read in her body language.

"You're a liar! You are just saying that because you're jealous! Jealous I have a man. You are bound and determined to make all men leave. I hate you. No one will love you," the mother shouted.

I wanted to hold the young girl in my arms and tell her everything was okay and that no man had the right to hurt her, but then I was pulled and found myself back at the front door again with the little boy and his dad.

"Go! Find your mother, stupid," the father said, kicking the young boy in the buttocks. The boy hurried to comply with his father's command.

I focused on the little boy and in a flash, was taken into the past again to his room when he was maybe only five years old. He was hiding under his bed, petrified. I watched as his dad entered the room. He went right to the bed and flipped it to yank the little boy up off the floor.

He held him in the air as he yelled at him. "You're so stupid! You think you can hide from me?" He hit the little boy. "Maybe this will teach you to respect me."

I was overwhelmed with emotion as I watched the little boy being hurt. How did he have a chance in this life, I wondered. But it was the past and I couldn't do anything to save him. My confusion about this whole experience left me feeling short of breath.

I retreated to my bench in the woods. I cried and tried to focus on surrounding myself in white light. It was no use. The deep emotions attached to everything I had just witnessed left me unable to tap into the light. *I can't do this. It hurts to see so much pain. I can't breathe.*

You can do this, Tallon. It was Michael. I was shocked to see him and stood up.

I can't, I told him. *It's awful. It's more than I can bear.*

You can do this, Tallon, Michael said again. *Your sensitivity is your strength. You have been chosen for this.*

I just want to be with my family, I cried.

He touched my shoulder. *I know,* he said lovingly.

But I don't understand any of this! I yelled at him in frustration.

Tallon, you are being presented with opportunities. You can do this. You need to fulfill your contracts the best way you know—allow the situation and its truth to be revealed. In that, you will see what you must do. But, as always, the choice is yours, Tallon.

And with that, he was gone.

I'm not special. I'm scared and uncertain of my path. Michael, don't leave me, please don't leave me, I called after him.

I felt so vulnerable in that moment. *How was this experience, how were these souls intertwined with my physical life? How did I let them down by taking my own life?* I wondered. Michael was right, the only way to know was to return to the house.

I was back in the kitchen. The little boy sat at a small table. It was now dusk. His father was sitting next to him with his chair positioned so he could look directly into the little boy's face.

"Tell us where River is, or you won't get anything to eat."

"I...I...d...don't know," the little boy said.

I noticed a woman who stood looking out the kitchen window, nervously chewing on her nails.

"Donna, what should we do?" the man asked.

"I don't know," Donna shot back, turning toward the boy. I realized this was the woman from the shed.

"Go walk around the neighborhood and down to the school and look for your brother. Then you bring him straight home! No fooling around, ya hear?" he shouted to the little boy.

"B...B...But it's almost dark."

"B...B...But it's dark." The father ridiculed him. "Your brother is out there in the dark because you didn't take care of him. Find him."

"I...I thought he was home," the boy said, crying.

"Lamar. Leave him alone," Donna said. "Maybe I should check again with the neighbors?"

"I will," Lamar said. He walked out the front door and Donna sat next to the boy.

"Why didn't you wait for River?" Donna asked.

"I...I thought he was home s...s...sick," he said. "I'm s...s...sorry, Mama."

"He ran to catch up with you right after you left for school. You didn't see him?"

"No," he whispered.

She sat up and gave him a piece of plain bread.

"Th...th...thank you, Mama."

This little stuttering boy had captured my heart. I just wanted to swoop him up and hold him forever. His little soul was so sincere.

"I saw him with you. You were holding hands on the way to school, Winter. Why aren't you telling the truth?" Donna interrogated him some more. "What happened? Just tell me the truth."

Winter. Did she say Winter? Oh, my God, this little boy is Winter? I had no idea he came from such an environment. He is so loving as an adult. You would never know he had suffered such abuse.

I thought of Winter, the loving man who had so willingly helped me in every way possible to reach Bryndle. As I thought about how he was a true friend, I was pulled to the present day in the living world. I found myself in Winter and Ruby's bedroom. Winter was tossing in bed as if he were having a bad dream. I entered his dream and could tell that he was having flashbacks from his childhood, of some of the memories I had just witnessed. It was as if his spirit knew I was in the past watching these events with his family. His dream shifted to him walking hand and hand with his little brother, River. They were laughing and smiling, and then River just disappeared. Winter looked everywhere for him, confused as to what happened. I jumped out of his mind and found him panting. Ruby could feel his anguish and woke up.

I loved how in tune they were with one another.

"Winter. Wake up," she said lovingly, as she gently shook him.

He sat up and cried in Ruby's arms. "Do you think I did something to River?"

"No love, I don't believe you hurt him. You didn't do anything. I know in my heart you were both victims of something."

"Why can't I remember?"

"Because, you're not ready, honey. Everything is okay, you're safe with me, and I know you didn't do anything wrong."

"What if I did, Ruby?"

"You didn't."

"But what if I did?"

"Then we will take care of it and get through it together, I will always be by your side. I know you, Winter. You are the kindest man I have ever known. You were just an innocent baby at the time. You could never harm anyone."

What is going on? I thought to myself. Winter was in turmoil and clearly had been since he was a child. He was full of guilt, anguish, and responsibility about what had happened to his little brother, River. I also felt his sincere confusion about the events that transpired back then. I had to find out the truth for my friend. I was obviously supposed to help him somehow when I was alive. In this realm, maybe I could still help him...perhaps by helping him remember what had happened? First, I had to go back and find out for myself.

I didn't say anything in the digital voice recorder that night because I didn't want to give Winter false hope or make him feel afraid or exposed because I now knew his secret. What if he did do something to his brother? That possibility just didn't feel like it matched the energy around the situation, though. I agreed with Ruby, but were we right? He had been a kid, after all, in a horrible situation.

I found myself once again in the past, back in Winter's kitchen. It was early morning, and two police officers now sat with Lamar, Donna, and Winter at the kitchen table.

"How long has he been missing?" one of the officers asked as he took notes on a small pad. This triggered my memory of the night Bryndle went missing. I remember the pure panic I felt, needing to find her and frustrated by the knowledge that we were wasting time as they tried to rule me out as a suspect.

"Like, yesterday morning," Lamar answered.

"When did you realize he was missing?" the officer asked.

"He was faking sick, that morning. He always does. He didn't want to go to school. At first, you know, we believed him. So, we said he could stay home from school, but told him he would have to stay in bed all day. He changed his mind at the last minute and decided to go to school. Winter had just left. River ran and caught up to him. Donna made sure they were together before coming back in the house. Winter came home from school at the regular time, but without River. In fact, he said he hadn't seen River all day. But we know that isn't true, because we saw him with River on their way to school. The teachers said River never made it to school, and no one has seen him since they walked to school together. I feel like everyone is lying to me about my son. I just want him back home," Lamar said, appearing deeply worried.

Winter just looked at the kitchen floor.

"Well, I wouldn't worry too much. In these types of missing kid cases, the kids normally show up. Do you mind if we look around?" asked the officer.

"Please do. We just want to find our son," Lamar said.

I focused on Winter. His little chin quivered as he sat at the table.

The police officers left the room with Lamar to look around the house.

"What did you do to him, Winter?" Donna asked. "Please just tell me."

"N...n...nothing Mama, I promise."

"You're lying. Dammit, stop lying! I know you were with him. I saw the two of you walking together to school. What happened?"

"Mama. He wasn't w...w...with me. He d...d...didn't come to school."

She pulled her arm back and slapped him across the face. "Don't lie to me, boy!"

He wept as the police officers reentered the room with Lamar.

One of the officers noticed him crying. "You okay, son?" he asked. Winter looked down and nodded.

"He says he doesn't remember anything. He doesn't even remember seeing River. Is that normal, officer? Do you think we should have him taken to one of those crazy hospitals?" Donna asked.

"Did you see River yesterday morning, son?" the officer asked Winter.

He nodded.

"Did he walk to school with you?"

He shook his head.

"Winter, I know he was with you! I saw him catch up to you, boy! You were holding his hand, damn it!" Donna yelled. "What's happened to my baby? Why is he lying?" She slammed her hand down on the table.

"He may not be, ma'am. I have heard of cases where the witness is so afraid, they can't remember anything—especially when it's someone they love. It might actually suggest foul play."

"So, he knows what happened to River, but can't remember?"

Lamar asked. "How do we make him remember?"

"Try not to put too much stress on him," the officer suggested. "I would take him to your family doctor and get him looked over. In the meantime, do you have a picture of River I can take to the station?"

"Yes, get the one off the fireplace, Donna. That's from this year's school picture. He's only six years old, officer, and he's been gone overnight now. We just want to find him. I have gotten pretty angry at this boy for not telling us what happened. I didn't realize he could have forgotten."

"Don't be too hard on yourself, you are just worried about your youngest son. We understand that. We all make mistakes when we're afraid. It's understandable," counseled the officer.

Ann and Michele Modtland

CHAPTER TWENTY-THREE

Finding River

THIS DIDN'T FEEL RIGHT. I couldn't understand what was going on and I was confused. What happened to River? Where was he? My instincts told me that Winter didn't physically hurt River. But what had happened? Was it so horrible that he had suppressed the memory? I couldn't help unless I knew the truth.

I sat down and focused on River. I imagined the little boy in the picture, on the mantle. Immediately, I was pulled to the rundown, abandoned house again in the present time. I was drawn upstairs to the boys' room. I inspected the bedroom from top to bottom, and I couldn't see anyone, but I could feel a child's presence.

The closet was the only place I had left to examine. *River?* I said softly, as I walked toward the closet. I peeked in the closet door and found a little boy curled up in a fetal position. He was in nothing but a dirty white T-shirt. River, honey, is that you?

The little boy looked up at me, surprised that I could see him. He had big, beautiful, dark- brown eyes, and I saw immediately that they were full of pain and loneliness.

It's okay, sweetheart. I'm not going to hurt you. I am here to help you, I said.

You are? he asked softly as he got to his feet. *But you're too small to fight the monster.*

I saw River's little face change from that of sincere inquiry to absolute fear. He turned his back and dropped to his knees to tuck himself as tightly as he could into the corner of the closet.

As he did, I felt a dark, strong energy from an entity right behind me. I could feel the evil in his intention. He wanted to trap me in fear and cause me pain. I quickly turned around and used my powers to throw him up against the wall and surround him in light. Simultaneously, I surrounded myself in light, afraid of the consequences if I didn't. I pinned his arms and legs to the wall. He fought against the light and yelled at me in a tongue I did not recognize. His face looked like a demon, and I wondered why he would want to present himself in such a fashion. He tried to push back with his darkness and strength, but he was no match for the light enveloping him and protecting me.

He was frustrated and his anger surged throughout the room. Next, he turned himself into a dark mass that appeared to dissolve against the wall only to change form into a little boy who looked exactly like the picture of River I had seen on the mantle.

Please don't hurt me. Please let me go. I just don't know who you are, and I am afraid, the little boy cried.

I hesitated. *Is this River?* I wondered.

He's lying. Don't let him go. He's a very bad man! The little boy called from the closet in a frightened voice.

I looked back to examine both their energy and determine who was telling the truth. The little boy was no longer in the closet. Then, I could sense River's fear coming from the other room where I assumed, he was now hiding.

I looked back at the wall where I was holding the dark entity in light. The form still appeared to be River, crying.

Who are you? I asked.

My name is River. I'm just so scared.

Who are you? I asked again.

River...River Boren. I'm just trying to find my family.

If you are River, then who is this little boy who hides in the closet?

A bad man. A demon. He keeps souls bound to this house.

Then why is he so afraid of you?

I wasn't sure who this entity was, but I was sure he needed to be dealt with. I could feel the innocence and real fear of the soul in the room behind me. I decided to keep this being up against the wall, pinned with light.

Give me your real name now. I will not release you until you do.

The truth was I didn't know what to do. I was afraid, but I needed to help River. The entity growled and hissed but couldn't escape the light. I continued my interrogation. *You, are a demon, aren't you? I will keep you trapped until I know who you are, and why you are here.*

He glared at me with hatred. The entity collected his energy and spiraled down toward the floorboards in a dark storm of movement. The tornado-like surge of energy clashed with the light, throwing me backward toward the closet door. I slammed against the door and slid to the floor. I looked up only to see the light was still holding him tightly against the wall despite all his efforts to break free.

Are you okay? the boy asked in a soft voice as he put his little hands on my face.

River?

He nodded vigorously. *I was wrong,* he said looking into my eyes.

What do you mean? I asked.

You are tough for your size. I think you tied him up good. But he will try to break free again, he said looking back at the demon.

River, can you tell me what happened? Can you tell me why you're here?

Are you an angel? he asked, avoiding my question.

I'm no angel, sweetheart, but I am here to help. How about we go downstairs and talk, I suggested, wanting to distance us from the demon and the events that had just taken place.

I got up and started walking to the stairs. The boy quickly followed and gently put his hand in mine. I looked down and smiled at him. This little boy already had my heart. I started making a list in my head of what I wanted to accomplish, a habit I have always done. I reasoned to myself that I needed to find the truth, to see if I could get River safely to the light, help the woman in the shed, and help release Winter from this horrific childhood mystery. As for the entity, or whatever that thing was upstairs—I would need help with that. Although I had a plan, I truly didn't know if I could accomplish it.

River, sweetie, my name is Tallon.

Tallon, he echoed.

Yep, Tallon.

I'm River, he said looking trustingly up at me.

I nodded in acknowledgment as I tried to figure out the best thing to say next.

River, can I ask you a question?

Yes, you can ask me anything, he said as he jumped down off the final stair.

Why were you hiding in the closet?

There's nowhere else to go. It's my only safe place.

Oh, I see. River, honey, do you remember seeing a white light?

Yeah, when I died.

Oh, you know you're dead? I asked.

Sure, I know, ma'am. You know you're dead? he asked, giggling.

Yes, I know. I couldn't help but smile as I looked down at him. He returned my gaze with a big, handsome grin. He was so cute and spirited. We entered the kitchen and I lifted him up on the counter.

When you saw the light, what did you do? Did you go into the light?

What did you do, Tallon? he asked as he played with his fingers.

I hesitated. *Well, sweetie...I didn't go to the light because, well, because I was looking for my spouse.*

I didn't go to the light either, Tallon, he said, looking up with his big brown eyes. Then he looked back down to his lap. *I ran away.*

How come? I asked.

Because, I didn't want to leave my brother.

Your brother?

My big brother, Winter. He's my bestest friend in the whole world. But they took him away.

Who took him, honey?

My grandma, she took him to live with her, but I wanted him to stay with me. We promised to always stay together.

Honey, what happened, how did you die? I inquired gently, with compassion and concern.

River just dropped his chin to his chest.

I know this is hard, River, but I can't help if I don't understand what happened. Can you be really brave now, and tell me everything? You saw how I locked that monster up.

River looked up at me.

You are safe now, sweetie, I promise.

No, he said, as he shook his head.

What do you mean no, sweetie?

My Mama is in the shed.

Yes, honey. Your mom is in the shed. Do you know why she is in there?

He shook his head as he rubbed his eyes with the back of his hand. *She's watching my body, so no one finds it.*

I looked out the kitchen window at the shed. *Your body is in the shed?*

He nodded.

Honey, I promise I will not let anyone hurt you anymore. Can you please tell me who hurt you?

He shook his head again, trembling as his eyes filled up with tears.

I love my Mama, he cried. *I can't.*

I realized I couldn't do this to him, couldn't keep pushing for an answer. I would have to find out another way.

Okay, honey. It's okay. You don't have to tell me. I wiped his tears from his face and gently kissed his forehead. *I am going to take you somewhere safe, okay? Can you trust me to do that?*

Yes, he said with a big beautiful smile.

Okay, just hold my hand.

As he placed his hand in mine, I focused on putting light all around us and took him to my safe place in the woods. We stood in front of the bench and I let out a deep sigh, relieved that it worked.

Michael, please let me see Bryndle. She is incredible with children and I need to get this baby to a safe place. Please, Michael. Bryndle, I need you, I called out.

River held my hand tightly and looked around to discover who I was talking to.

A white light manifested to our right and my beautiful Bryndle, holding our Oryan, appeared right in its center. She walked toward us, looking radiant. She embraced me and then looked down at River and smiled.

You got him, Tallon, you got him, she whispered softly and then bent down. *Hi River. I'm Bryndle and this is Oryan.*

Hi, River said, smiling shyly. He tried to hide behind my leg. He was interested in the baby and watched her every move. I could tell she had grown a little already. Oh, to see my family again. To have them there with me in that moment meant so much. As a family, together we were always able to figure everything out. I looked at Bryndle inquisitively as she seemed to know all about River.

I watch out for you, you know, she said with a smile.

Of course, you do, I said, kneeling next to her as I kissed her cheek. *I need your help, honey. He's a good little boy, and he's been through so much. He isn't ready to talk about it, but he deserves to be in a safe place as I try to figure it all out. Can he stay with you and Oryan?*

Just then, Michael walked out of the light and noticed River.

You gained his trust. Impressive, he said.

River, do you want to come here on this bench to play with Oryan? Bryndle asked. I knew Bryndle was trying to give me a chance to speak with Michael alone.

No, thank you, ma'am, he said, holding my hand even tighter.

I looked down at River and gave his hand a squeeze and winked. I looked back up at Michael. *I personally know his brother, Winter. I'm sorry but I couldn't leave River there. Something evil is there. I'm not sure who or what it is, but this little boy has been trapped there long enough.* I looked at Bryndle, adding, *I just wanted to get him to the safest place I knew.*

Michael just nodded and River looked up at me when I mentioned his brother. Michael moved closer and looked at River and then at me.

Tallon, I came to assure you that you did the right thing, he said, smiling with approval. *I will be back.* He disappeared.

Bryndle smiled and handed Oryan to me. It felt so good to see her and to know she was with Bryndle. It meant everything.

I knelt at River's level. *This is my baby girl, River, would you like to say hi?*

Yes, he said, taking Oryan's little hand. *Oh, she is so cute, but so small! We will need to protect her from the monsters.*

It's okay, sweetheart, there are no monsters here, Bryndle assured him.

No monsters? he asked, looking at me.

Nope, no monsters in heaven, buddy. You will be safe here forever, I said.

But what about my brother, you said you know him? River asked.

I do and he's safe. I promise.

The light reappeared, and Michael returned with a man and a woman.

They approached River. *River, my name is Michael and I want to introduce you to your family. This is your mom's great-grandmother, Ida, and your dad's great-grandfather Henry.*

River hesitated as he looked up at me, again holding tight to my leg.

I know you don't remember them, but they have been waiting a long time to meet you, Michael told River.

The man and woman introduced themselves. *We are so happy to see you, River,* Ida said. *We will take care of you. We would love to have you come with us.*

River shook his head, refusing.

I am sorry for all you have suffered, River. I know it will take time for you to trust again, Michael said softly.

River kept looking fearfully at his great-grandparents.

I understand you're not ready yet, River. But could you do me a favor? Will you come to the light with us, and help us care for Oryan? Michael asked. River's eyes widened with joy and his smile grew. I wasn't sure why River was hesitant to go with his family, but he already cared for Oryan and wanted to be near her. I knew Michael had a plan.

River looked at me. *Can she come too?* he asked.

Oh, River honey, I can't come yet. I have some work to do. I need to help your brother. I can promise you that your great-grandparents and

Bryndle will take good care of you. And Oryan needs a big brother to help watch out for her.

Bryndle placed a hand on his shoulder. *That would make us so happy, sweetheart. Oryan would love having a big brother.*

I kissed Oryan and gently handed her back to Bryndle.

But Winter, what about Winter? I want my brother.

I could feel his pain and knew he needed to see his brother. I looked at Michael. He nodded and walked back into the light. River and I stood near the bench.

River, you know you were hurt, right?

Yes, he said, his little body quivering with emotion.

And you know that Winter wasn't hurt, right?

He got hurt, but not hurt to death, River whispered.

Okay, honey, but you know you died, right, and that Winter is still living?

He sobbed. I held him on my lap while he cried, wrapping him in my arms, and kissing his forehead.

Sweetheart, I am so sorry for what happened to you, but you are safe now, I promise. I still had no idea what had happened to this little guy. *I promise you, River, that no one will hurt you again. Honey, did Winter ever hurt you?*

No, he said, firmly. *He never hurt me. He's my brother, my bestest friend.*

I held him close, pressing his head to my heart. River was so adorable and tender-hearted. How could anyone have hurt him?

Your brother is all grown up now, River. In fact, he's a dear friend of mine, I told him.

He is? Did he teach you to play closet house? Where you are always safe and it's warm with lots of food?

We never played much, but I am sure he is lots of fun to play with. He has a wife now and kids of his own.

He's not that old, River said, laughing at me.

River, about how long have you been dead?

I know I missed Christmas.

I rethought my plan of showing him Winter. He clearly couldn't fully understand. I smiled at him.

So, I have an idea. Why don't you go with your grandparents and Bryndle so we can keep you safe, and where you can play with Oryan. Would you do that for me?

But I am still there in the shed. I can't get me, he said, confused.

Oh, your body. Are you talking about your body? I inquired.

He nodded, as big tears ran down his face.

Well, if you stay here, I think you will have fun. I will go take care of your body. Then you never have to go back there unless you want to.

Okay, he said. Loving light surrounded us. *But where are we, Tallon, and where is Winter?*

This is heaven, buddy. Where people love you and no one hurts you. Winter is safe but he can't come to heaven yet. I am sure you will be able to talk to him soon, though. I know he has been thinking about you.

He has? I miss him so much.

He misses you, too, but now you will be safe, and all he wants is for you to be safe.

Okay. Will I see him again?

Yes, sweetie, you will see him again. I promise.

And if I go with them, the monster won't be able to find me?

No monsters are allowed in heaven, remember? Do you like stories? I asked, changing the subject.

River nodded.

Bryndle tells the best stories, and I am sure your great-grandparents know some incredible stories, as well. As I touched the end of his nose with my finger, Bryndle and his great-grandparents stood before us.

Are you ready to come with us, River? his great-grandfather asked. *There are lots of kids to play with in heaven.*

River nodded and let go of my hand. He walked toward his great-grandpa, and then turned back to me, still needing reassurance.

It will be okay. I promise. I will see you again soon. I winked at him. He smiled and took his great-grandpa's hand. His great-grandfather nodded to me in gratitude. I watched as they walked toward the light.

Bryndle walked close and gave me a hug.

I love you, Tallon, I love you more and more every day, she said, kissing me. *You're incredible and I am so proud of you.*

I love you, Bryndle. Thank you for helping me. I kissed her goodbye and bent down to kiss Oryan.

Stay strong. Everything will work out, my love. We will be watching you, she promised. Then she and our beautiful baby daughter returned to the light.

CHAPTER TWENTY-FOUR

Cutting the Darkness

I WANTED TO GET word to Winter, to let him know his baby brother was safe, but I wondered if that would be premature. There were issues I needed to address first, questions requiring answers. I wanted to do right by River and uncover the truth. The uncertainty of whether to tell Winter or not weighed heavily on my heart. I thought about what I knew and, most importantly, how I felt about Winter and his possible involvement.

I knew River had said that Winter had never hurt him, but I didn't have any answers as to what really had happened to River. These kids experienced an abusive childhood. It was possible anything could have happened. My mind raced. I couldn't make an informed decision in this state. I sat down on the bench, in full lotus position, and meditated. Calling upon my higher self and quieting my mind, I allowed my soul to lead me. I felt I needed to tell Winter, regardless of what may have happened in the past.

I figured the best way to share this delicate information with him was to go see Raya. I was a little nervous in approaching her, as I had no idea how she had been doing these past few months. I prayed she would be able to hear me. When I arrived, I found her in the garden pulling weeds. It was a beautiful day to garden, and I wished for a second that my hands could feel the soil and that my body could soak in the sun just one more time. Life—what a priceless gift, and when we are living, do we ever really understand how precious it truly is?

Raya, I said gently, hoping she could hear me. Nothing. *Raya,* I said again with more force. She didn't even flinch. She had no clue I was standing right before her. Why was she still preventing herself from hearing spirits talk? Hadn't she made any progress with her mentor? I felt so bad knowing that she still felt responsible for my suicide, especially since she wasn't. I was. And I haven't regretted it.

I felt a deep connection to Raya, and I kept thinking about what her mentor said about our souls having a spiritual contract—but honestly, I wasn't sure what that meant. However, I was aware that Raya had brought so much peace to so many people with her gift, and I knew the world needed her.

Raya! I shouted as I attempted one more time, but she just continued gardening. Feeling hopeless and ridden with guilt, I became emotional and just started talking to her out loud.

Oh Raya, I know this is ridiculous because you can't hear me, but I have so many things that I need to say to you. I want to apologize for the pain I caused you. I'm sorry that I hurt you. None of this is your fault. You had the courage to tell me the truth. Most people wouldn't have been brave enough. With the information you shared with me, you gave me the opportunity to help Bryndle from the other side. You helped me save my wife. Did you hear that, Raya? We saved her. What happened was meant to be. On the spiritual side of things, you did nothing wrong. Please, release all the guilt, and embrace your God-given talent. You bring peace to so many people.

I just watched her for a minute, as she pulled more weeds. I reasoned that even if she couldn't hear me, part of her could feel my energy and intent. *We did it, Raya. We helped Bryndle, and now she is with my grandma, her parents, and our sweet baby, Oryan. I have to do some work,* I explained. *Suicide has implications, as you well know. I could really use your help in all of this. I can feel that you are part of this bigger picture, too.*

Raya turned toward me and briefly looked in my direction but didn't acknowledge me. *Hmmm, how am I going to help you realize that I am here? An act you can't deny, but something that won't scare you too much.*

I looked around the garden for a minute, and then I found what I was looking for. I picked up her bucket of weeds and waved it in front of her face. She stood up, surprised, and a bit more afraid than I had intended her to be. In her moment of fear, Raya's natural response was to call upon her spirit guides for help, and with that extra help and support, she could finally see me.

"Tallon, is that you?"

I smiled at her.

"Tallon, could that really be you?" she cried. I heard her spirit guides update her on Bryndle's status and my present path. She stared at me. "Tallon, it's really you, and you did all this to save Bryndle?"

Yes, Raya, and I'm afraid I need your help again.

"Okay, of course. So, I helped you and the info I provided didn't lead you to commit suicide?"

I did it to save Bryndle, and she's safe now. I saw her absorbing what I was saying as if she finally had found redemption in knowing the truth. She sat down on the grass, relieved to know she was not responsible for my decision to take my own life.

Raya, I know this is a lot to take in right now, but if possible, I really need your help.

"Why, yes, of course."

I have found Winter's little brother, River. He passed when they were both just young boys. I am not clear on what happened yet, but when it's time, can you help them to connect?

"Of course. You reached River? I have been trying to reach him for years on behalf of Winter. I would love to, providing I still can. Tallon, I've been so closed off, thinking that I hurt you. I don't..."

Her spirit guides assured her that as long as she's open to it, she can utilize all her gifts again. Raya smiled and nodded her head knowingly. "So, Tallon, my spirit guides inform me that you are helping souls move to the light now, and you are responsible for bringing Bryndle's murderer to justice in the physical world."

Yes, that's true, and I never would have embarked on this journey if not for you. I touched her arm lightly to send the message home.

"Wow. Tallon, that is unbelievable. Look at how much you have grown spiritually. You vibrate with a strong but loving energy, like nothing I have experienced before. It's like you are physically here, Tallon."

I am physically here, I shot back with a smile.

"You know what I mean," she laughed. "Tallon, please know that I am always here for you, to help you in any way. Thank you for coming back and giving me this gift and for understanding."

I would do anything for you, Raya. Thank you for everything. Thank you for being strong enough to tell me the truth about my wife.

She wept, and I put my arm around her shoulders to console her. I saw her husband pull up into the driveway on his motorcycle. As he climbed off his bike, it was obvious to him that his wife was talking to someone he couldn't see. He smiled with relief.

For me, it was time to focus back on the task at hand. I returned to the old abandoned house and went upstairs to the boys' bedroom. My fear dissolved as I witnessed the evil entity—or monster, as River called him—still pinned up against the wall. However, to my surprise, he appeared drained and weak, most likely from his consistent struggle to break free of the light. His head hung down with exhaustion, but as I approached him, he looked up. I gasped and covered my mouth with my hands. He was in his true form, most likely unable to shape-shift due to his lack of energy.

Lamar? I questioned in shock.

Let me go. Please let me go, I beg of you, he pleaded, as his body shook.

No, I need some answers first. What really happened to River?

That boy never made it to school! That boy was always mixin' up trouble! He just never made it home. Winter did something to him. That boy was worthless! He took my son from me.

Why are you binding River here, to this house in the spiritual realm if that is the truth? Tell me the truth.

That is the truth, he insisted.

I could feel his dark energy. This man was a liar and felt no compunction in deceiving me.

Now, please. Please have mercy on me and let me go. I'm the victim! My son was taken from me!

I shook my head in disgust, and out of frustration, walked out of the room. If he wasn't going to tell me the truth, I would go elsewhere.

Wait! Where are you going? Get back here! You can't do this to me! Release me! he yelled.

I decided to go back to the shed. I closed the door behind me and walked up to Donna. I found her in the same corner of the shed, curled up in a ball.

Donna, I said firmly.

She turned around and sat up, shocked that I knew her name. I was learning that there is power in knowing a spirit's name, the name they had in life. It takes away some of their power, their ability to deny and deceive.

I found River.

No, you didn't, she said and quickly glanced at the ground. *No one will ever find my baby.* She distorted her face and hissed at me.

In the core of my being, I knew my next step was to make sure River's body was found. Perhaps just as in Bryndle's case, if I could resolve the situation in the living world by exposing secrets, then healing in the spiritual world could begin.

I went to see Detective Cunningham. He was in his office doing paperwork. I started talking out loud to him, forgetting that few people in the living world can hear me.

He was engrossed and didn't move. As soon as I realized what I was doing, I rolled my eyes at my foolishness and walked to his computer. I typed. *Hello, it's Tallon.*

"Tallon," he said with an enthusiastic, but low voice as he quickly glanced outside his office window into the hallway. "I wasn't sure I was ever going to hear from you again."

River Boren's body is in the shed, under the floorboard at one three two two Snow Canyon Drive. Behind the abandoned house.

"River Boren?" he asked. "Who is River Boren?"

I searched his computer database for unsolved cases, not certain how far back they went. Detective Cunningham sat and watched, as he kept checking the hallway, to see if anyone was looking. His breathing quickened. "This still kind of freaks me out, Tallon."

I couldn't find anything on this boy, *Not in here. Is the case too old? River Boren went missing on May fourth, nineteen sixty-nine.*

"Yeah, nineteen sixty-nine. Old cases like that wouldn't have been scanned into the system. If we're lucky, we might still have a hard copy of the case down in the dungeon."

Next, I did a search on Lamar and Donna Boren. Both had records for drug use and public intoxication. Both were deceased, Lamar from a drug overdose and Donna from an apparent suicide.

"Okay, Tallon, I'll look into it and see what I can find," he said, trying to talk without moving his lips, paranoid that someone was watching. He made me laugh.

Find his body, so he can be laid to rest. River is Winter Boren's little brother.

"Okay, Tallon, I've got it," he said as he pushed his chair away from his desk. "And next time you take control of my computer, can you please save what I am working on," he chuckled, as he got up from his chair.

I turned the lights off and on in his office to joke back with him.

"Don't do that. Seriously," he said as he bolted to the door. "Would you like to accompany me downstairs?"

I turned the light off and on again to let him know that I would.

"Tallon!" he yelled under his breath.

I couldn't help but giggle as I followed him out into the hall.

Stacy was right outside his office door. "Why are your lights always turning on and off? I'll have maintenance look into it," she said, handing Detective Cunningham a file. "Here is the file you asked for on the Finch case."

"Oh, thank you, Stacy. Do you mind leaving it on my desk?" We walked hurriedly down the hall toward the stairs to the basement.

"Okay, Tallon, assuming you are still with me. This is the room where we keep the cold cases." I was surprised at how many boxes were stacked in the room, completely unorganized and covered in dust. I couldn't help but feel emotional at the thought of knowing how many families never got answers or justice for crimes that were committed against them. It also made me wonder how many souls might be stuck in-between worlds. I was overwhelmed by the realization of how large that number could be.

Detective Cunningham worked his way through file boxes. I focused on River, and in the back of the room, I felt something connected to him. Allowing it to pull me, I followed the energy source to the end of the aisle where I found a glowing box. I pulled the box forward and blew off the dust. *Could this be it?* I wondered.

Detective Cunningham heard the movement and walked in my direction. I kicked the box to verify that I had caused the noise he heard.

"Tallon, is that you?" he said, as though startled. "I'm too old for this, even though I know it's you, it's still spooky. Because I guess it's logical to believe if there is one of you then there are more. I can see it now, a ghost leading this whole cold case operation." He laughed nervously. "Okay let's see what you got here."

He opened the box and there was a missing person's report on top for River Boren. In the file was a single piece of paper containing a handwritten police report. It detailed the parents' account of the whole event. Winter's version of not remembering seeing him that day was included as well, with the words, possible suspect. The description of what he was last seen wearing, differed from what River had been wearing in the closet. I couldn't believe it. A five-year-old disappeared, was never seen again, and there were only a couple of lines to account for it? It seems Detective Cunningham felt the same.

"That's all? A five-year-old boy disappears, and this is all the investigation entailed? And there doesn't appear to be any follow-up report. I hate to admit it, but in nineteen sixty-nine, in this area the disappearance of an African American boy would have been put on the back burner. Damn it! This is wrong and we need to make it right."

He grabbed his radio and made a call to dispatch. "I have received an anonymous tip that a missing boy's body is buried in a shed behind an old abandoned house on Snow Canyon Road. I need a team dispatched immediately." He gave them the address. "I need to open an official case."

I stayed with him as he did. I appreciated Detective Cunningham so much. The fact that he trusted me to this extent was both unbelievable and wonderful, especially when I needed his help to bring closure to a soul on the other side.

We got in his car and headed in the direction of the old abandoned house. His cell phone rang. "This is Detective Cunningham...I'm on my way, wait for me to get there."

"They just arrived and are in the process of securing the property, Tallon. Let's get this boy some justice."

Without thinking, I grabbed his arm in a gesture of appreciation. My touch caught him by surprise and the car swerved. I reminded myself I need to remember that people can't see me.

"Damn it, Tallon," he shouted nervously. I couldn't help but laugh hard at his reaction. "If you need to tell me something, can you use this?" he said and chuckled as he put his cell phone down on the console.

We sat quietly for the next few minutes of the drive. In my heart, I knew Winter needed to be there when they dug up the remains of his little brother. He deserved closure. I touched the cell phone, and with a little manipulation, I managed to get to a blank messaging screen.

Winter should be here, I texted.

He picked up his phone and looked at what I had written.

"Okay, but...we don't even know if this is River, or if there's a body for that matter," he said, shaking his head. "Well, you know its River, don't you?" he added ruefully. "I'll send a car to pick him up."

Satisfied, I left Detective Cunningham's car and went directly to the shed. Police cars and vans surrounded the property, and the shed had been taped off. To my surprise, standing off to the right-side near the front of the house were River, his great-grandparents, Michael, and some other spirits I didn't recognize.

I entered the shed and Donna was there in the corner, upset about the commotion outside.

Donna, they are here for River, for his body, I said.

What have you done? she yelled. I wasn't sure what was going to happen next, so I took a few steps back. She lunged at me and tried to tackle me, but I moved out of the way just in time, and she fell to the ground. She spun around and was up on her feet in seconds. I knew I needed to stand my ground. *They are coming, Donna, whether you like it or not. So just tell me what happened so that I can help you.*

Realizing the reality of the situation and that it was finally over, even if she somehow could dispose of me, she dropped to her knees and sobbed.

No one can help me, not now.

The next thing I knew I found myself in the past, on the morning River went missing. River was lying in bed clearly sick and fighting a fever. Winter was right by his side, putting a cold washcloth on his forehead.

"I'm so w...w...worried about you, little brother. You feel s...s...so hot." Winter said as he felt his brother's cheek.

Donna entered the bedroom. "What are you boys doing? Stop fooling around. You are going to be late for school!" she screamed, as she slapped Winter on the side of his head.

"But, Mama, R...R...River is sick, and he had an a...a...accident."

"You wet the bed again!" Donna yelled.

Lamar heard this and entered the boys' room. "Did I hear you wet the bed again, boy?"

"I'm sorry Daddy, it was an accident. I don't feel good," River apologized weakly. His body was damp with fever, his skin pale.

"I'm tired of your accidents!" Lamar yelled, yanking River out of bed.

"Your mom is not washing your sheets anymore. You're not a baby," Lamar said, gathering up the sheets and throwing them at River. "Go wash your own bedding!"

"But I don't feel good," he pleaded. His large brown eyes begged for help.

"He has a f...f...fever, Mama. I'll wash his sheets." Winter bundled the sheets up in his arms.

"No, River has to learn." Lamar yanked the sheets from Winter and threw them back at the younger boy.

"Are you sick, River?" Donna walked to River and placed her hand on his head. "He is hot, Lamar. Go get another cold cloth, Winter." Winter happily headed out of the room to get a cloth when Lamar stopped him.

"He's lying. Aren't you, River? Every time you wet the bed you have an excuse, well your excuses are over," Lamar said.

"Lamar, I think he's really sick. I don't mind washing his bedding. Do we have any fever medicine?"

"How dare you disrespect me in front of my boys!" he shouted, slapping her in the face. The boys froze.

"I'm not, Lamar, I didn't mean to. I'm just saying I think River is really sick."

"You think I don't know my own boy?" he yelled. They all knew how fast things could escalate. Donna retreated in fear. Lamar, still enraged, continued slapping and began punching her.

"You stupid bitch. I won't allow any son of mine to be a bed wetting, lying, disrespectful kid. You're the worst mom ever. You're lucky I don't just leave you."

"D...D...D...Daddy, please stop," Winter pleaded as he inserted himself between his father and mother to try and protect Donna.

"I'm sorry, Daddy!" River yelled, to get his father to stop hitting his mother. "I'm sorry, I lied Daddy."

Lamar stopped. "See, I told you he was a liar. Now get my belt." He pushed Donna out of the room.

"No, Daddy, please, please, I'm so sorry, Daddy," River begged Lamar.

"I...I...I w...w...will...," Winter struggled to speak.

"I, I, I," Lamar taunted him. "You are so pathetic, get your ass to school, Winter. I have to teach your brother a lesson."

Winter held his brother close, trying to protect him, but Lamar ripped them apart and shoved Winter down the stairs. Winter ran back into the room as Donna entered slowly with the belt.

"Please, Daddy, no, I won't wet the bed again, I promise," River pleaded.

"I...I...It was me D...D...Daddy, I wet the bed," Winter said, trying to take the blame.

"I told you to go to school! Get him out of here!" he yelled to Donna.

Donna grabbed Winter by the arm. "You best get to school, son, or it will be worse for us all. River will be on his way soon."

"But, M...M...Mama?"

Donna pushed him out the front door as the sound of a belt whipping against River's body echoed through the house. River screamed for his dad to stop. Winter tried to get back inside, but Donna had locked the door. She remained leaning against the front door crying as she listened to the screams of her youngest son.

"Winter, just go!" she yelled from inside the house as Winter pounded on the door.

A group of kids were walking by the house on their way to school. Winter turned away so that they could not see him wipe away the tears and the streaks of blood resulting from the blows he took as he tried to protect his mother.

I watched as Winter took a few deep breaths to get control of his emotions. After a few minutes, he walked to school, looking back at the house every few steps, as if torn by the decision he had been forced to make. My heart broke for him. He felt so responsible for caring for and protecting his brother. The amount of abuse these boys suffered was indescribable.

I watched, as a distraught Winter trudged all the way to school. He walked alone, with his head hung low, his mind consumed by the morning's events. As he approached the schoolyard, the bell rang.

"Oh no," I heard him say under his breath as he ran to his class. When he entered his classroom, everyone turned and looked at him.

"You are late again, Winter. I gave you so many warnings," his teacher said scornfully. "Why can't you ever get to school on time?"

"I'm s...s...sorry, Mrs. Howard," Winter said, lowering his head.

The kids in the classroom laughed and made fun of his stuttering. To my astonishment, Mrs. Howard didn't correct them and turned Winter's desk around to face the wall. "Have a seat, Winter. Maybe this will help you learn how to be on time."

Winter sat starring at the wall, alienated, harboring a secret, a deep worry for his brother's safety. His shoulders trembled, as his chest rose up and down as he gulped each breath, trying to fight showing his tears.

I was choked up, hurting inside for this little guy. Every adult failed this child, let him down in every way. I wanted so badly to hold Winter and save him from this pain, but there was nothing I could do about the past. I looked out the classroom window when it dawned on me that I had accompanied Winter all the way to school, and River never joined him like his parents had told the authorities. They lied. So, what had really happened? I immediately returned to the house.

As I was warping, I felt a strange pull from Emi. I could feel her thinking about me. I felt horrible, but I couldn't go to her. I needed to stay and find out what happened to River. I made a mental note to check on Emi as soon as everything was resolved here.

Back at the house, River had endured a fierce beating from his dad. He was stiff and sore. His back was bleeding from the belt and I watched him struggle in pain as he washed his sheets in the kitchen sink. His white T-shirt was sticking to the fresh wounds on his back and was turning red from the oozing blood.

"Get up here, River," Lamar yelled.

Donna was in the kitchen making sure River was cleaning the sheets properly. "You better go see what he wants, I'll hang these on the line."

"Thank you, Mama." River ran up the stairs as fast as he could.

Lamar was standing in the bathroom. "You learn your lesson today? Donna, get in here, too!"

Donna hurried into the bathroom.

"River will learn how to pee in the toilet today," Lamar said, smacking River's head. "Now, sit on that toilet, and we will be checking to see if you go in it."

River sat down on the toilet.

"Now go, pee in the toilet," his father commanded him.

River sat there.

"Why don't I hear anything?" Lamar asked.

"I don't have to go potty, Daddy."

"Oh, you don't? Is that because you like to pee in your bed like a baby?"

"No, Daddy..." he gasped when Lamar punched him in the stomach.

"You are sitting here until you learn to go to the bathroom in the toilet, do you understand?"

Hours passed and River, deprived of food and water and his fever spiking, continued to sit on the toilet. Several times an hour, Lamar entered the bathroom, getting more and more angry each time when he saw that River hadn't used the toilet. I knew the poor little guy was most likely dehydrated from his fever. Each time, Lamar punched or slapped River as punishment.

"Mama, Daddy, can I please go to my bed now. I don't feel good and my legs hurt." River's body was shaking from his fever and from the trauma of the beating he was receiving. He coughed up blood but kept wiping it away for fear that he would get in trouble for not being tough enough. I saw that this baby was used to bleeding.

"No, River, you can't go to bed until you use the toilet," Donna yelled.

"But I'm so cold, Mama. Please. Please, let me go to bed," he pleaded as he cried even harder.

"Stop crying like a baby!" Lamar said angrily as he came back. "You will sit there until I say you can leave, do you understand?" He yelled at him and punched River in the stomach again.

Donna walked up the stairs to see what was going on as River fell to land on his hands and knees on the bathroom floor, gasping for air.

Lamar laughed as River struggled to breathe.

"Look at that, he's learning, ain't he," Lamar handed Donna a half-empty bottle of whisky, and she took a drink.

"Yeah, he's learning all right," she said. "Maybe we should let him go to his room?"

"Get back up on that toilet," Lamar ordered, ignoring Donna.

"I'm sorry, Mama. I'm sorry, Daddy. I love you, please." River cried, quivering as he lay on the floor struggling for breath. He tried to sit back on the toilet when his body finally collapsed. His eyes glazed as I saw blood hemorrhage from his mouth and his breathing stop. His last bit of life left his body and his spirit hovered above, watching his body.

"Get up!" Lamar yelled.

"You better get up, River, you will only make it worse, son," Donna said nervously.

"Get up!" Lamar shoved River's body with his foot. "Get up, boy! I said, get up!" He lifted River's arm only to have it drop unresponsively.

Donna glimpsed River's lifeless eyes, she realized he was gone. "Wait! Wait!" she screamed. "Oh, my God, Lamar, you've killed him!" Donna shoved a shocked Lamar out of the way and grabbed for her son. She collapsed, rocking her son's body, back and forth sobbing. "My boy, my boy, dear God, my boy."

Stunned and confused, Lamar took River's body from Donna. "He's just faking," he said as he put River down on the floor and watched for a breath, but it never came. Lamar slowly stood up and backed against the wall, staring at River's still body. Donna again rocked her son as she wept for what they had done.

"We need to call for help. You killed him. Get help!" Donna pleaded. I saw River's spirit, still standing in the bathroom, looking at his body. He was so confused. I tried to talk to him, but this was in the past, and he couldn't see me.

"It was an accident. You killed him, too. He wasn't tough enough. This isn't our fault," Lamar said, trying to justify River's death.

"What are we going to do?" Donna cried. "We need to call someone for help."

"Do you want to spend the rest of your life in prison? 'Cause that's what they will do, they will blame us."

"Blame you," Donna corrected.

Lamar grabbed her and shoved her against the wall.

"You did this, too, and unless you want to end up like River, you best help me come up with a plan," Lamar threatened.

Petrified, Donna could only nod in agreement. "What should we do?" Donna murmured.

"We need to get rid of the body first and then come up with a good story," Lamar said calmly, coldly. "We can say he left for school and never made it home. The cops aren't going to look into it that much 'cause we're black. It happens to our kids all the time, especially in these parts. They don't care."

Donna again held River close to her chest. "What have we done? What have we done to my baby?"

River's spirit walked toward his body. Light surrounded him. Then, I heard him say, *I got to find Winter*, and he ran away from the light and retreated to his bedroom closet.

I followed his spirit into the bedroom and watched as he came out of the closet and went to look out the window.

He watched as his parents carried his body into the woodshed. Then, I watched the many hours they spent trying to convince Winter that River was with him that morning on the way to school and that he had to know what had happened to his brother. I was pulled back to the shed—it was present time and Donna was still protecting the spot where her son's body was buried.

Donna, I know what happened to River.

She turned and looked at me.

They are coming for his body, Donna.

No, they aren't. No one can find his body as long as I am here, she snarled at me.

Donna, this is your chance to make things right. I know you feel bad about what happened to River. You have an opportunity to take responsibility and allow River to rest in peace. Do the right thing, Donna.

It's too late, she said, crying.

I could hear the forensic team planning to enter the shed and begin digging for River's body.

Donna, they are here, and they are coming to get River's body.

How would I even begin to do the right thing? she asked, finally showing some remorse.

Let them recover River's body. I don't really know what happens next, but I know the first step is taking responsibility for your actions and allowing the truth to manifest.

I didn't mean to hurt my baby. I should have stopped it. I was too weak, she confessed. Donna wept huge sobs that seemed to rise from the depths of her soul.

I reached out and held her hand. I knew she had been through so much. I thanked God that I didn't have to judge, because actions are far more complicated then I could even begin to comprehend.

God must hate me, she said. *I suppose I deserve to go to hell. You're right, I want to take responsibility. I owe that to my son.* And she stood up.

I closed my eyes and mentally called for Michael's assistance. The truth is, I personally didn't know what to do next.

I heard a voice from behind me. *Are you ready, Donna?* Michael asked.

Yes, she said, hesitantly preparing herself to face the truth. Two angels came in and carried her away. She screamed and cried as they left the shed. She looked down as a heavy black energy cuffed itself to her hands and feet.

Is that necessary? I asked.

She's cuffing herself. She is allowing her guilt to do it. She believes she deserves to be in chains and will punish herself greatly for what she has done, for what she allowed to happen. She will punish herself even more than anyone else could, Michael explained.

Where are they taking her? I asked.

She will do her work, wherever she believes that it should be done. It differs for everyone and is a personal choice. As she does her work and begins to heal, the places she chooses to stay will most likely change. Of course, eventually she will have an opportunity to come to the light. However, some avoid the light—that much love makes them uncomfortable. In addition, to come to the light, she will need to fully understand the consequences of her choices and take complete ownership for what she did in life. She will feel everything she did, and every way in which she caused pain. It may well be more than she can bear. She will always have a choice either to stop or to continue in her growth and healing. She will have to accept forgiveness, as well. It's a loving process, and completely up to the individual. If she is committed to healing, she will regain her true light.

How long does it typically take? I asked.

It's up to her. Depends on how willing she is to take responsibility and how much love she allows herself to hold.

What about Lamar? He's still upstairs?

Well, Tallon, he is refusing to go, refusing responsibility and refusing to feel loved. He has been released—you can't bind a spirit forever. He will most likely roam the earth until he is ready.

But can he hurt people? I just couldn't understand that he still might be able to harm other people.

Possibly, but it's his freedom to choose, Michael said. *One day he will no longer have the choice to remain on the earthly plane. Tallon, I must leave now, I'm here to support River and his family.*

As Michael left, I heard Detective Cunningham approaching the shed.

"Okay, break the lock on the door and let's start digging."

They didn't have to dig for long before they came upon a shallow grave under the shed floor. Winter and Ruby stayed all night, watching the events unfold. I could sense their overwhelming pain, mixed with relief, as little River's body was exhumed.

I watched as River's great-grandparents held him and supported him throughout the process. When River saw me, he ran up and hugged me tight. *Thank you, Tallon, thank you so much.*

Do you know who that is there? I asked.

He smiled a huge smile. *My big brother.*

That's right, Winter is here because he loves you. He never stopped looking for you, River. I wanted him to know that Winter had never left him.

The following week, a small funeral service with close family and friends was held for River. It was beautiful, with blue and white flowers blanketing his grave and a large statue of an angel standing guard as his headstone. Winter, Ruby, their kids, and some of their extended family, along with Detective Cunningham, Raya, and my parents were all in attendance. Donna was there, as well, in her self-imposed chains. She had asked to attend but buried her head in shame during the whole service.

Raya, comfortable again with all her gifts, approached me following the service.

"Hello, Tallon, how are you holding up?"

Good, Raya, thank you. You are looking well again.

She gave me a big smile.

How are they doing? I asked, nodding toward Winter and Ruby.

"They know everything, Tallon, and they are so grateful for your help."

Well, I am grateful for all their help, too, I said quickly.

"They wanted me to let you know that they are retiring from the EVP business, handing it to one of their students. Now that River has been laid to rest, they want to just enjoy being grandparents. Their oldest daughter is expecting her first baby, a little boy, and they are going to name him River." Raya choked up as she relayed this information to me. "But they have an EVP recorder connected to a computer in the office, so if you should ever need anything, or if they can help in any way, they want to support you. They have a lot of love for you, Tallon...and of course, deep down they still love the EVP business." She smiled.

Have you talked to my parents by any chance? I am shocked to see them here.

"Well, I know Detective Cunningham had a long talk with them and told them how you helped to solve this case and helped to bring this little boy to peace. He's so proud of you and he knew your parents would be, too." Raya nodded. "And they are, Tallon."

I stood there and took in all Raya had told me. I was so lucky to have such loving parents. Even after my death, they went out of their way to support me.

As if Raya could read my thoughts, she spoke again. "Yes, they love and adore you and Bryndle and Oryan. They hurt deeply that you are all gone but know that you're all okay. They are so proud of you, Tallon, and the decisions you have made to reunite your family. I'm surprised you didn't know they all talk about you...although, I suppose you're busier than most spirits.

"And, Tallon, please allow me to help you in any way I can, as you embark on your path. Because looking back, helping you, as confusing and emotional as it was, was the first time I really felt like I was in the right place, doing what I was meant to do."

Then, I saw her stare over my right shoulder.

"Tallon, is this Bryndle and the baby?" she asked as she reached out to touch my arm.

I could feel them behind me, and I turned around with a big smile to greet them.

Yes, it is. I put my arm around Bryndle and greeted Oryan. *This is my wife, Bryndle, and our beautiful baby girl, Oryan. Bryndle, this is Raya, the woman who helped me understand you were in trouble and needed help.*

Bryndle handed the baby to me and put her hands-on Raya's shoulders. *It's so great to finally meet you. Thank you for helping to save me. You have no idea what it means to me.*

She gave Raya a big heartfelt hug.

Raya welcomed the embrace. "It is so good to see you and Oryan safe, united, and happy."

The next thing I knew, I found myself back at my bench in the woods with Michael, Bryndle, Oryan and my grandmother standing before me.

You have an incredible gift, Tallon. You are needed in the spiritual realm, Michael said.

Thank you, Michael, I replied humbly.

Tallon, you don't quite understand what I am trying to say. I had sent several Deliverance Angels to River, and we had spent years trying to gain his trust. And with Lamar...no other newly returned spirit has been able to bind an earthbound entity like you did. There is something special about you, Tallon. It will be interesting to see where you choose to go from here.

I looked at him, perplexed.

I know you don't remember yet, but it has been your longtime dream to be a Deliverance Angel, Michael continued. *I feel with the abilities you have already shown, we should give you a little more deliverance training, in addition to your current work completing your contracts. But, it's up to you. A part of your soul has always been encouraging you to accept lessons and challenges toward this goal.*

Deliverance Angel? I asked.

Yes, God will never leave a soul alone—and although many things can keep a soul earthbound, a Deliverance Angel is always nearby to help, when appropriate.

Why didn't Bryndle have a Deliverance Angel? I asked.

She did. But she needed the right one, just like River.

As they prepared to leave, I knew Michael wanted me to ponder his words. I hugged them all and said goodbye once again. The sting of our goodbyes rang through my soul, and I wondered how long it would be until I never again had to say goodbye to my wife and child.

Missing my family, I decided to check on my little brother. He was sleeping when I arrived, and it gave me so much peace and comfort to watch him. He had his action figures all around his room, and his favorite ones right next to him on his nightstand. A large photo of all my family hung on the wall above his bed and a paper directly below it was written, *Family forever, RIP, I love and miss you Tallon, Bryndle, and Oryan.*

I looked back at his little face and kissed him. Chewy was sleeping at the end of his bed and woke up to greet me. I petted his head and whispered, *I love you, too, buddy, thank you for taking such good care of my brother. I sure miss you both.*

He stood there wagging his tail with excitement.

"We miss you too, Tallon," Odin said as he sat up in bed rubbing his eyes.

I'm sorry, buddy. I didn't mean to wake you. I just wanted to tell you how much I love you. Lie back down and let me tuck you in. It was just like old times when I was alive.

"I love you too, sis," he said as he lay down.

I didn't want to leave, but I could feel a soul needing me. I kissed him on the cheek and whispered to him. *Sleep good, buddy and tell everyone that I love them. And Odin...*

"Uh-huh," he said with his eyes closed.

Just say my name if you ever need me. I am always watching over you. I love you, little brother. Goodnight.

"I love you," he said and called out to my parents as I left. "Mom, Dad, I saw Tallon, she says she loves us, and goodnight."

CHAPTER TWENTY-FIVE

Unwanted

I RETURNED TO MY bench and enjoyed the sound of crickets in the moonlight as I waited for the soul I felt to make itself known. I saw movement out of the corner of my eye. It was a small figure, moving from tree to tree. I tried to focus, attempting to decipher what it was, but it was moving so fast, I was unable to identify it.

Who's there? I asked hoping it was a who and not a what.

Behind a large pine tree, a little girl—about five years of age, with long dark hair and big dark eyes—peeked out.

Hello, why don't you come out and talk to me? I said softly.

Okay, she answered and walked to me.

She had an interesting sense of style. Her hair was unkempt and had random braids scattered throughout. She also sported a large white feather hanging from one of her braids. Her clothes looked old and worn. She wore a tie-dyed T-shirt and cut-off shorts. She had mismatched shoes and on her right foot she wore a single, long white tube sock with two orange stripes at the top. Judging from the mud stains on her attire, she clearly loved nature. From her neck, a pinecone hung from a piece of purple yarn. Although adorable, she appeared completely uncared for.

Is this your place? she asked.

Yes, I guess you can call it that, I replied.

This is your bench? she asked, running her hand admiringly across it.

Yes, I said, hesitantly, as I realized for the first time that my name and photo had been added to the bench.

And this is your family?

Yes, they are.

Wow, you must really be loved, she said, as she skipped around the clearing.

Yes, I suppose. What's your name? I asked her.

What's your name? Wait, I know your name. It's Tallon.

How do you know that? Oh, did you see my name on the bench?

I can see your picture, she replied, and I realized she probably couldn't read.

I saw what you did, she said.

What do you mean, you saw what I did?

How come you left toys at this tree? she asked, standing in front of the pine tree. *Is it so you would have toys to play with when you crossed over?*

No, we left them to show love to my daughter who had passed.

Wow, no one has ever left me anything. Your daughter, I don't remember seeing a girl. How old was she?

Well, she hadn't been born yet.

Oh, your wife was the pregnant woman who was murdered. They took your baby right away. That man made me leave the woods. He scared me. I came back for the girl's camp on the other side of the falls. One of the girls left this necklace behind. She held up her pinecone necklace. *Can you believe she would just leave it?*

It's pretty, I said.

People always leave cool stuff behind. That's how I got these shoes, she said with a smile. *Could I play with these toys?*

Sure, of course.

What is this? she asked, picking up one of the robots that Odin had left.

It transforms. Let me show you.

She handed me the toy and immediately sat down in front of me, interested to see what I was going to do with the toy. *See, it changes from a car into a robot.*

Wow, that's cool. If I could transform, I would change into a bear. A bear?

Yes, a bear. Everyone loves bears. They are always sleeping with them and giving them as gifts. Bears get lots of love.

Oh. I realized she was talking about stuffed teddy bears. *That is true. So where is your place?*

Here in the woods. I like it here, especially in the summer. Lots of people come here.

I used to love coming here in the summer, too.

I know.

I looked at her with renewed curiosity. *What's your name?*

Why aren't you with your family? she shot back.

Because I did something that I need to make right.

Yeah, I saw what you did.

You saw what I did?

Yes, didn't you like your body?

I loved my body, I answered and then it clicked. She had seen me kill myself.

Didn't you like your life?

I loved my life.

Then why did you do that to your body?

Because...it's hard to explain, and no one should ever do what I did. You saw what happened to my wife, right?

I was hiding.

Well, she was so afraid, she didn't go to the light, so I ended my life so I could try to help her.

Because you love her?

Yes.

That's weird. Do you miss your body?

Sometimes.

I just don't understand why people get rid of their bodies. Did you like having a body?

Yes.

Have you ever ridden a bike?

I have, I said, smiling at her curiosity.

That's so cool. Have you crashed? Did you bleed? Did it hurt? Once I saw this boy crash and his whole leg was bleeding, and he cried, she said before I could even reply.

It can hurt, I admitted.

Yeah, I thought so, but at least he got to ride a bike. He had a cool helmet with a Mohawk on it and everything. It did look scary. What's bubblegum like? Have you had ice-cream?

Um, bubblegum is chewy and, yes, I have had ice cream.

Wow, you have done lots of things.

I have. What did you do when you had a body?

I listened to my mom's heartbeat. It was amazing. And I could hear her talking sometimes.

Sweetheart, what's your name? I asked.

She looked down as if ashamed. *I don't have one. I'm an unwanted.*

An unwanted? I asked, not certain what she meant.

Yes.

So, does that mean you don't have a name?

I wasn't given one, she whispered as she looked the other way.

What would you want your name to be? I asked

Naming yourself doesn't stick. I've tried. One time, I tried to name myself Moonlight Horse, but nobody would call me that. You need to be loved to be named. Someone who loves you has to name you, isn't that how it works?

I suppose, sometimes. All I could do was just listen as I tried to figure out her heartache.

That's how it works, she instructed me as if I was unclear about the rules. *Have you met the deer in the clearing?*

Um, no, I can't say that I have.

They are so nice. Sometimes they let me sleep with them. And they are really great at keeping secrets, too.

I leaned in toward her and, making eye contact, I spoke softly. *Sweetheart, what do you mean you're an unwanted?*

My mom didn't want me. I'm an unwanted. It happens. Have you ever seen a trapeze show? she asked as she balanced on one leg. *I once delivered a guy who fell from a tight rope. He was really nice but just didn't want to believe he was dead. I was like, you've passed. It's okay, it happens. He had a huge funeral and everything. I held his hand and walked him to the light. He thought he wouldn't be welcomed to the light because he smoked, isn't that silly?*

Why aren't you in the light?

At first, 'cause I wanted to be with my mom. The light is full of the unwanted. I know my mom wants me because sometimes she thinks about me in her dreams. But then, it was souls calling me, needing my help. So, Michael made me a Deliverance Angel. I guess I'm supposed to train you. Michael says you need a lot of help, she announced as she balanced herself across a log, mimicking a tightrope act.

Oh, really? I asked, still perplexed. Michael had mentioned training, but I didn't realize I was getting an actual trainer, and a five-year-old one at that.

How long have you been a Deliverance Angel?

A long time. You know what I don't get? What's so bad about getting old? Why doesn't anyone want you around when you get old?

People are still wanted when they get old.

Not most people. Most old people are lonely and hurt in their hearts. I don't like delivering them as much, because they've become unwanted too, and it really hurts my heart.

I guess people forget how much they love them sometimes and life gets busy.

Yeah, that's stupid.

You said you wanted to be with your mom? Why did you want to stay with her if she really didn't want you?

Because I love her. And I know she loves me, too. She just doesn't know me yet. One day, she will be so happy to know that I am hers.

I am sure she will.

She makes me laugh. My mom is amazing. She likes pizza. Have you ever had pizza?

I have, and I like it, too. I winked at her.

She likes to run, even when no one is chasing her. Most people don't like doing that.

I smiled. *You mean she likes to exercise?*

Yes, that's what I mean, exercises.

I felt Emi pulling me again. This time more urgently than before. I can't believe I hadn't checked on her yet.

Do you feel that? the little girl asked.

Yes, I do feel that.

That's my mom. I have been trying to reach her all week, but she won't listen. She's calling you. She's in-between.

Who, Emi?

Yes, Emi. My mom.

Ann and Michele Modtland

EPILOGUE

Life in Death

MANY PEOPLE THINK OF death as a permanent slumber or a heaven where you gain instant knowledge and the gift of a forever life. But there is so much life in death, so much work to be done. Death has presented me with opportunities to grow and expand my love more than I had ever imagined. Things aren't what we had been led to believe while we were on earth. We all have choices and I am making a conscious effort to choose love. I would challenge you to do the same, regardless of the realm you reside within. For all the answers are found in love.

My given name is Tallon Monroe, and this is the story of my life in death. If you should ever need my help, just call my name and I will answer.

About Ann & Michele Modtland

Ann & Michele Modtland have been married for ten beautiful years. Michele graduated with honors from the University of Utah with a Bachelor of Science in Psychology. Ann is artistic and loves to crochet and express herself through works of art. Ann and Michele currently reside in Utah, enjoying the life-changing experience of raising their daughter, Jersey, whom they adore and are teaching to live in a world without labels. Their profound love for animals keeps them involved in several animal rescue efforts. Presently, the Modtlands have the privilege of sharing their lives with five dogs and three cats.

Connect with …

Email: modtlands@gmail.com
Facebook: Ann & Michele Modtland

Note to Readers:

Thank you for reading a book from Desert Palm Press. We have made every effort to edit this book. However, typos do slip in. If you find an error in the text, please email lee@desertpalmpress.com so the issue can be corrected.

We appreciate you as a reader and want to ensure you enjoy the reading process. We would like you to consider posting a review on your preferred media sites and/or your blog or website.

For more information on upcoming releases, author interviews, contest, giveaways and more, please sign up for our newsletter and visit us as at Desert Palm Press: www.desertpalmpress.com and "Like" us on Facebook: Desert Palm Press.

Bright Blessings